KT-212-447

The Time of Green Magic

HILARY MCKAY

MACMILLAN CHILDREN'S BOOKS

Published 2019 by Macmillan Children's Books
an imprint of Pan Macmillan
The Smithson, 6 Briset Street, London EC1M 5NR
Associated companies throughout the world
www.panmacmillan.com

ISBN 978-1-5290-1924-7

Copyright © Hilary McKay 2019

The right of Hilary McKay to be identified as the
author of this work has been asserted by her in
accordance with the Copyright, Designs and Patents Act 1988.

All rights reserved. No part of this publication may be reproduced,
stored in a retrieval system, or transmitted, in any form or by any means
(electronic, mechanical, photocopying, recording or otherwise),
without the prior written permission of the publisher.

Pan Macmillan does not have any control over, or any responsibility for,
any author or third-party websites referred to in or on this book.

1 3 5 7 9 8 6 4 2

A CIP catalogue record for this book is available from the British Library.

Printed and bound by CPI Group (UK) Ltd, Croydon CR0 4YY

This book is sold subject to the condition that it shall not,
by way of trade or otherwise, be lent, resold, hired out,
or otherwise circulated without the publisher's prior consent
in any form of binding or cover other than that in which
it is published and without a similar condition including this
condition being imposed on the subsequent purchaser.

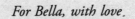

For Bella, with love.

Salt Spray and Shadows

T here were no curtains at the window and the room was bare, except for the sofa and Abi's rocking horse and Abi herself, hunched over her book like a diving bird on the edge of a pool, poised between worlds. The grey late afternoon was cold, but Abi didn't notice because in her book the sun was blazing hot, even in the shade of the big, creaking sail. Judging by the amount left to read, the journey was about halfway through.

Abi turned the pages slowly, not wanting it ever to end. She was crossing the Pacific Ocean on a raft made of logs, rush matting and rope. Out in the ocean, buffeted by the lively wind, everything was moving: the long waves, the glinting reflected light, and the giant, rolling balsa-wood logs. There were no clouds. The enormous sky fitted the enormous ocean like a great blue basin, turned upside down. The basin's rim was the immense circle of the horizon, sky blue against sea blue.

Every now and then Abi looked up, to absorb the perfect roundness of that horizon, squinting to see against the brightness and salt wind. Everything was salty. Her lips tasted salty. Salt spray had twisted her already curly black hair into tight salty springs. They blew into her eyes and stung. She pushed them aside, hardly noticing, and read deeper and deeper.

Her name was Abigail, but only Granny Grace called her that. Everyone else called her Abi. Reading was Abi's escape. She read while other people cooked meals and loaded dishwashers and swept floors. She read while her father dragged into her life Polly as stepmother, plus two entirely unwanted brothers. She read through the actual wedding ceremony. She read while Granny Grace flew away, back to Jamaica, a trip postponed for ten years while she helped bring up Abi. She had read through the year that followed, squashed with three strangers into a too small house. Most recently she had read through the start of a new school.

But she had never read a book like this.

It was a hardback, with a faded blue cover. *The Kon-Tiki Expedition*, read the tarnished silver letters on the front. It was old-fashioned – she had skipped loads – but the bits she had read were entrancing. Lately, it had begun to have a sound to it, a soft echo when you opened the pages, like the ocean sound in a seashell.

Abi read: '*We were visited by whales many times. Most often they were small porpoises . . .*'

There was a parrot, bright green, always curious, never in the same place. It flew down towards her, swerved away at the last moment . . .

2

'Abi, Abi, *Abi*!'

Abi jumped so hard she would have fallen if she hadn't put out a hand to save herself. Her book did slip. She grabbed it just in time.

'Abi, I can't see you!'

'Here on the sofa,' said Abi, blinking, half dazzled by Pacific sunlight.

'There was . . . What was that green?'

'What green?'

But Louis had already forgotten. It had been no more than a wing tip, a fan-swirl of green parrot feathers; it had flickered into Louis' vision and left no imprint as it vanished.

Louis vanished too. Abi was alone in the quiet room again. It felt strange to be back, to look around and notice that the light in the room was autumn faded, and the wind had ceased to blow. She rubbed her eyes, and found them stinging, then cautiously tasted a tip of a finger.

Salt.

CHAPTER ONE

In the beginning (and ever since her mother's car crash when she was just a year old), Abi had lived with her father, Theo.

Granny Grace, Theo's mother, lived with them too. Granny Grace had been going to take a break from her work teaching and visit Jamaica when the accident happened, but she never did. She said she'd rather look after Abigail instead.

At the same time (and ever since their father had decided he'd rather have no children and live in New Zealand), Max and Louis had lived with their mother, Polly.

Abi and Theo and Granny Grace lived happily in a small sunny flat in one part of the city. Polly and Max and Louis lived just as happily in a small terraced house in another.

These two sets of people didn't know each other.

This all changed one afternoon when Max and his best friend Danny were in a fixing-things mood and took apart their skateboards, cleaned out the gunk from the wheels and the axles, put them together again, and sprayed all the moving parts with expensive lubricating spray borrowed without asking from one of Danny's big brothers.

Then they went outside to try them, and Louis went with them to watch.

'They should go much faster,' said Danny, and he dropped his board on to the pavement and gave a mighty launching-off kick, and the front wheels could not have been fixed back on properly because Danny went hurtling down on to concrete paving slabs just as Max got into action. Max's wheels stayed on, and his board was now spectacularly fast. Max mowed down Louis and went straight over Danny before he too hit the ground.

Then Polly, hearing the roars, came rushing out of the house, and when she saw the boys all bleeding and wailing and blocking the pavement, she unhesitatingly took them to hospital in the old blue car she had painted herself, with the tiger cushions in the back. Louis had two skinned knees and a lump on his head like a great dark purple plum. Danny and Max had a broken arm each and various lesser injuries, but the chief thing that happened at the hospital was that Polly met Theo. Theo was the nurse in the Accident and Emergency department who oversaw the management of the skateboarding calamity. He did it with such admirable cheerfulness and calm that very soon the injured ones stopped feeling like woeful victims, and became instead very pleased with themselves, fine adventurers and heroes all.

'Thank you so much for popping in,' Theo said at last, six or seven hours later and pitch dark outside, when all the bandages, slings, plasters, and stickers saying how brave people had been, were finally in place.

'It's been lovely,' said Polly. 'I've enjoyed every moment.'

Then Theo's smiling eyes gazed into Polly's sparkling ones, gazed and gazed and gazed.

'Do you believe in love at first sight?' asked Theo (unprofessionally).

'Yes,' said Polly. 'I do.'

That was how the two families met, and a few months later, when Abi was eleven, Theo and Polly married each other.

'Oh, my!' said Granny Grace. Not at the start, though. When she'd first met Polly, she'd been awful about the thought of a stepmother coming into Abi's life, but by the time of the wedding things were different. 'A little bird has told me your Polly is a wonder,' said Granny Grace. Granny Grace's network of little birds stretched all around London, and even back into the past. They knew everything and were infallible. She trusted them completely, so she'd finally come round.

'Oh, my!' said Granny Grace, after much communication with many little birds. 'Can it be that my work here is done at last?'

Never once, throughout the whole ten years that Granny Grace had lived with them, had she mentioned that long-postponed trip back to Jamaica. Suddenly she couldn't hide her joy.

'Did you know she wanted to write a cookbook with her sister?' demanded Abi of Theo. 'That she owns quarter-shares in a beach cafe and they are going to rebuild and relaunch with a whole new menu? Did you know she has so many nieces and nephews, and that they all have children she's never seen? Did you know she inherited a cat that lives with her friend? Or how much she has missed Jamaican flowers? She'll never come back!' lamented Abi.

'Then we'll visit her,' said Theo. 'And meet the cat and eat at the cafe and learn the names of the flowers and admire all the babies.'

'Just me and you?'

'And Polly and the boys – they'll love it. Don't gaze up at the sky like that!'

'Well!' said Abi.

'Abi, Abi,' said Theo gently. 'You know, and I know, that Granny Grace deserves every happy moment.'

The next great change was that Theo and Abi moved into Polly and Louis and Max's house.

Then there were difficulties. The way that thirteen-year-old Max suddenly found himself sharing a bedroom with six-year-old Louis, which meant he entirely stopped inviting friends home and spent endless hours at their houses instead. The eye-rolling awfulness for Max and Abi (Louis didn't care) when Theo and Polly, for instance, held hands. Also Abi's problem with Louis, who had assumed little-brother rights much too fast. Louis continually forgot that his old room was now Abi's. He wandered in unannounced whether Abi was there or not, and he always seemed surprised to find himself unwelcome.

'I'm getting *dressed*!' Abi complained one morning.

'I know,' said Louis, unmoved.

He was a fragile, bony, pale little boy, with sticky hands always eager to reach and grab, or hug or hold. Baths and showers made little impact on the permanent grubbiness of Louis. His clothes never fitted, his mouth never quite closed, his blond tattered curls dangled over his eyes and as often as not housed nits. Nits! Abi had caught them and the treatment had been terrible and, afterwards, her hair! Polly had helped, and Theo had helped, but the person who could have helped most was thousands of miles away: Granny Grace, whose deft, quick fingers had for ten years twisted Abi's hair into woven braids and topknots with no apparent effort at all.

'You need a professional,' Granny Grace had dictated from Jamaica and commanded a trip to a hairdresser. That had solved the problem, and Polly had remarked, 'Next time, we'll know what to do.'

'There won't be a next time,' Abi vowed, and she had had to become very stern with Louis. 'Knock on the bedroom door, and then wait! . . . Put my bag down *now*! . . . No, I won't look at your horrible knee! And you shouldn't kiss people with your mouth full!'

On top of Abi's Louis problem, there was her intruder-feeling problem.

'A new, ready-made family for us, Abi,' said Theo. 'I always worried that you were an only child.'

'I still am an only child!' protested Abi, although silently, in her head. (She found herself doing a lot of silent protesting

9

in her head these days.) 'But now I'm an only child in someone else's house!'

Abi had felt like that from the start, in the kitchen with its cupboards full of other people's food and mugs and plates, and in the living room where she never knew where to sit. Even more, in her new tiny bedroom where she could not even escape with books without feeling guilty, because she was the only one with a room of her own.

'Thank you,' said Abi stiffly, when she first heard that Max and Louis were going to double up and share.

'Mum made us,' said Max grimly. 'I suppose we'll get used to it,' he added, sounding like he didn't believe it for a moment.

Abi didn't believe it either. Great quarrels came erupting from behind that bedroom door. Louis, although utterly messy in his appearance, was obsessively tidy in his room. Max was the opposite. Max lived in a great heap of Max-junk. He and Louis stuck a line of tape across their bedroom floor, dividing the enormous Max-mess from the extreme neatness of Louis. Nothing could stop Louis seeing over the line, though, just as nothing could save Max from having to listen to Louis droning himself to sleep at night, like an out-of-tune mosquito.

The rocking horse was yet another problem. He was no ordinary rocking horse; he was one of the full-sized, galloping sort, capable of catapulting a child some distance over his head when going at full speed, and foot-crushing and shin-rapping on an almost daily basis. Before Abi, he had belonged to Abi's mother. Abi, who had parted with so much – her bedroom, her home, Granny Grace and nearly all her past life – had become silent when it came to what to do with Rocky. Not stubbornly silent, just plain miserable silent. And in the end Rocky had moved too.

Louis had been delighted.

'Rocky isn't a toy – he's an antique!' Abi protested, finding his saddle smeared all over with chocolate. 'What have you pushed in his mouth?'

'Banana for his breakfast,' said Louis unrepentantly. 'Can I glue a horn on his head so that he can be a unicorn?'

'No you CANNOT!' said Abi. 'Leave him alone! Why do I have to share *everything*?'

'You don't share anything!' said astonished Louis, and Abi, equally astonished, had only just managed not to growl, *What about my dad?*

There was no space for Rocky in Abi's new tiny bedroom, so he lived a wandering life until he ended up in the hall, squashed against the coats, taking people by surprise (and once knocking out a tooth). After the tooth problem (which had happened with one of Louis' friends) Theo said, 'Abi, don't you think . . . ?'

Polly rescued her. Polly said it was only a first tooth that would have had to come out anyway very soon, and that she, personally, had organized extra compensation from the tooth fairy, and had paid in advance.

'Thank you,' said Abi, and Max, inspired, stuck a notice on

the front door: BEWARE OF THE ROCKING HORSE, it said.

It was the first joke anyone had made for some time.

After that, very gradually, all of them living together began to be more bearable. Louis was just as grubby, Abi was still very quiet, but Max stayed at home slightly more, and the quarrels and negotiations became less frequent and noisy. And then, one March morning, a letter arrived in a long white envelope.

Polly read it and handed it to Theo, and their eyes met again, very worried this time. Polly said, 'I'm sure it's nothing to worry about, but . . .'

(At the word 'but' Louis, who was a worrier, felt an invisible line trace down his spine, as if drawn with gritty chalk.)

'. . . this house is rented and the owner wants it back . . .'

'So?' said Max.

'So we're not going to be able to live here much longer . . .'

Abi, with whom the being-silent habit had stuck, drew in her breath very suddenly, and they all noticed, the way people notice when leaves begin to move after a stillness in the air.

'Not live here any more?' Louis asked in such a doomed voice that Max explained, 'Mum means we're going to have to move house.'

Louis, after glancing from face to face, checking he was hearing right, exclaimed, 'But it's stuck to the ground!'

*

12

'Moving house doesn't mean you move the house!' said Polly. '*We* will move, to another house.'

Louis couldn't imagine how this could possibly be achieved. Did you one day just walk home from school to a different place? And then, did a new door open, and that was home? Did you take your stuff, or was that cheating?

They hurried to reassure him. You took your stuff.

'Everything in the house,' said Polly. 'Nearly. Not the carpets. Or the fridge. The washing machine, but not the cooker. It'll be fun! An adventure!'

An adventure, but not the cooker.

'The taps?' asked Louis.

'There'll be new taps,' said Theo.

Louis sighed with relief and asked, 'Where?'

Where became everything. They house-hunted on the internet, and on the streets and in estate agents' windows, and they asked people-who-might-know, and nobody ever did. They lost track of the number of places they visited, where the neighbours looked scary, or the traffic was endless, or the garden (if there was a garden) was a rubbish heap. The local schools to those houses were either much too posh or looked like prisons.

Weekend after weekend, with more and more urgency, they searched. They stood in strange hallways and glanced uneasily at each other and the air smelt alien. Packing had already begun at home, and Louis wondered aloud about the possibility of packing air. Home smelt of toast, Polly's lemony perfume, damp coats and the fern on the windowsill. After some thought Louis fetched a shoebox and carried it from room to room, scooping it full. Then he took it outside, lifted a corner of the lid and sniffed, taking care not to let much escape.

It didn't work. It smelt of shoebox.

'Not of home,' said Louis. 'Not a bit.'

'No,' agreed Abi, for whom home had smelt quite differently, of cooking and coffee mostly, drying laundry and running shoes.

'What'll we do?'

'You'll have to put up with it,' said Abi.

'Put up with it?'

'Bear it,' said Abi. 'Bear everything different. Like I did.'

Bear it, wondered Louis. First the cooker, and the taps (although there would be new ones), now this new worry. He had grown accustomed to Abi not talking, the way he was accustomed to trees not talking. Now suddenly the words were back. Very startling words too. *Everything different.* What next would Abi announce in her hardly used, slightly husky voice?

'I've found a house,' said Abi.

They were in yet another estate agent's, and it was late in the day. Polly was in charge. She had marched in, determined, saying, 'A house is a house. We are being far too fussy.'

Then she had been far too fussy herself, instructing them,

'We're renting, not buying, so we don't need to bother with places for sale. Louis!'

Louis, who had begun running in small circles, changed to jogging on the spot.

'Please, Louis!'

Louis sighed, and slumped down beside Max, who had found himself a sticky, squashy, plastic-covered seat and taken out his mobile phone.

'Can I play a game on it?' asked Louis, without much hope.

'No,' said Max, so Louis allowed his spine to become boneless, and trickled down the gap in the back of the chair.

Abi looked at the FOR SALE displays that they didn't need to bother with, and found a house half built of leaves under a pointed roof.

'I've found a house!' she said again, and this time very much louder. 'Here!'

'Nope,' said Theo after a single glance. 'Not possible! It's not for rent. Besides, look at all that ivy!'

The estate agent (who knew, by the condition of their shoes and the hunch of their shoulders, the exact income and state of mind of everyone who arrived through his door) now came over too. As a matter of fact, he said, the house was actually for sale *or* to rent, and the ivy made it a wonderful bargain. 'Insulation,' he explained (he had been trying to get rid of the house for a long time, and what with the ivy and other things, it was proving a very hard job). 'Insulation,' he repeated. 'And – of course – green!' Then he pressed a house brochure into Polly's hand.

15

'Oh no!' she exclaimed after one startled look. 'Too tall. Too narrow. Too many stairs. Rooms stacked like boxes on top of each other. And much too much money!'

'Hear, hear!' said Theo.

'Oh dear,' said the estate agent, and he gazed at them as if they were a problem family, so that Polly, feeling judged and guilty, looked at the brochure again and said, 'Of course it would be perfect, in a way, but the cost! And anyway that ivy must be full of spiders!'

'Not at all,' said the estate agent, suddenly sounding as confident as David Attenborough, 'because of facing north.'

Theo and Polly looked at each other with the faces of people who know nothing about spiders or facing north but are damned if they will admit it.

Louis demanded, 'Are we staying here all day?' from his carpet-smelling cave, and Theo said, 'Absolutely not,' so they went and looked at other places.

The other places were all so awful that by evening they deliberately drove home by way of Abi's house to prove that it really was impossible.

It was at the bottom of a street that ended in a dark bank of yew trees and it was like no other house they had ever seen. It had coloured glass in the windows and an arched front door.

'We might as well get out for a minute,' said Theo, so they did, and stood with their heads tipped back, straining to see the peak of the pointy roof. The house was so tall and narrow that this was difficult.

Ivy covered the house, right up to the top. The front and

the visible side were entirely green. Louis pushed his hand deep into the leaves to feel the warm brick underneath.

Beside the front door was a lantern straight out of Narnia: wrought iron and glass panels. Abi found a light switch, half hidden amongst leaves.

'The electricity will be off,' said Polly, but Abi tried it anyway, and suddenly the lamp glowed golden, like a promise or a blessing, shining down on their upturned faces, melting all their hearts.

There was a thin new moon in a pale green sky. Traffic whizzed past at the end of the road but the street itself was quiet.

'It's beyond us completely,' said Theo and Polly sadly, and turned off the lamp, herded everyone into the car, and drove away.

There was nothing on the internet, nothing. They searched all evening, going mad. Then they went back to the estate agent and got the key to the ivy house.

'How can we rule it out completely if we don't look inside?' asked Theo, excusing this insanity.

Inside, the air smelt of long ago. The stairs were the sort you fly down in dreams. The coloured glass in the hall windows seemed full of accumulated sunlight. In this house, thought Abi, it felt that nothing could be impossible.

Eventually, one by one, they drifted apart, exploring, opening doors, pausing by windows.

'There'd be room,' said Polly, 'for Abi's rocking horse.' And she spoke like a very tired person seeing the end of a journey.

'Room here,' said Theo, 'for half a dozen rocking horses! A flock! A herd! What's the word for a lot of rocking horses?'

'A rocketing,' said Polly, and then she and Theo sat down on the stairs and began working out how much they could afford if they worked much harder and kept it up till they were ancient and never had any emergencies, holidays or extra children.

Abi went to count the rooms. The kitchen was the biggest, with old-fashioned cupboards and a huge battered table. There was also a sitting room with wooden panels right up to the cobwebby ceiling, and an instant waiting silence when she opened the door. She discovered the boys in the attic bedrooms, which were up two flights of stairs. Louis had spotted a wooden box in a corner. It was locked, but Max found a key on the windowsill.

'Treasure,' wondered Louis hopefully.

'Books,' Max said, disappointed, when he got it open. 'This can be Abi's room, because of the books.'

Abi's room, Abi heard. A room of her own again, where she had a perfect right to be. Hers, because she liked books. 'Yes, this can be my room,' she said aloud. She turned the books over, one by one. They were old, faded hardbacks with mottled pages, about half a dozen, perhaps.

'Nobody reads stuff like that any more,' said Max.

'I will,' said Abi. 'If we move here. I wish I could help.'

'Help?' asked Max.

'With money,' said Abi, and she began collecting together her treasures in her thoughts. How much were they worth,

18

and could she part with them? Not Rocky, of course, but her silver charm bracelet (no, NO! But yes, if necessary). Her Lego pirate ship that had taken a whole year to assemble, her signed Harry Potter book, her collection of Jamaican seashells, her book token and her very small pine tree that she had grown herself from a pine-cone seed.

Max was not going to be outdone by Abi. He thought of his savings: nearly a hundred pounds in pocket money, birthday presents and uneaten school lunches. He'd known they would need it one day. And it would be worth a hundred pounds not to have to share with Louis.

Louis said urgently, 'Listen!'

'What?'

'No, listen!'

The house with its ivy sighed and creaked around them.

'Gone,' said Louis at last.

'What was it?'

Louis shook his head, not wanting to say, so Max finished giving out the bedrooms. Book room for Abi, and the one next door for himself. Square bedroom on the floor below for Polly and Theo, and smallest room next to it for Louis. The window of that room was particularly deep in ivy, and when Louis pushed it open to admire his view he heard a sound like a question: 'To-who? To-who?'

'There!' breathed Louis. 'That's what I heard before! A nowl.'

Theo and Polly heard the owl too.

'Is this house what you might call . . . eerie?' asked Polly.

'Yes,' said Theo.

'Yes,' agreed Polly. 'I'm glad it's not just me.'

'Bound to be,' said Theo. 'So old. The ivy. Nothing wrong with a bit of eer! It's not like there's poltergeists throwing things at your head.'

Polly shivered, and then got up from the stairs and went to peer at the garden. 'It's been let go wild. What's behind those yews? Oh . . .'

'Quiet neighbours,' said Theo, who had already worked out that the churchyard was next door, and hadn't known whether to mention it.

'What?' asked Abi, suddenly appearing, and Theo told her, 'Just seen, behind the yew hedge . . .'

'Oh,' said Abi. 'The old churchyard.'

'Doesn't it put you off, Abi?' said Theo, raising his eyebrows. Abi shook her head. 'Could we move here?' she asked.

'We've got to move somewhere,' said Polly, clutching her ears, as she did in times of stress.

'I can help. There's my signed Harry Potter. We could sell it.'

'Oh, Abi,' said Theo.

'You can use my hundred pounds if you need it,' said Max, who had followed Abi down.

'There was a nowl,' said Louis, from the landing above. 'A nowl,' he repeated, pushing past them all, and tugging open the front door. 'Listen!'

'To-who?' came the question again, faintly from beyond the yew trees, and Louis on the doorstep whispered, 'To me! To me!'

Abi came to stand beside him. She heard the huff and whine of traffic at the top of the road, a faint radio from the noodle shop on the corner, the rattle of an empty crisp packet blown in a gust of wind, car doors, her own heart, a rustle from the base of the yew hedge and the slam of a door.

No owls (or nowls), but, once, a wheezy croak.

'Would you like to live here?' she asked Louis.

'Not on my own,' said Louis, alarmed.

'No, no, with all of us.'

'All right,' agreed Louis, and then, without warning, took off and ran inside.

Abi lingered after he had gone, listening. The owl called again. The Narnia lamp shone on the breathing ivy leaves. There was a smell of flowers. Abi hunted in the half-light until she found them, white bells on thin wiry stems amongst spear-shaped leaves. She took a stem inside.

'Lily-of-the-valley!' exclaimed Polly when she saw them. 'When I was little . . . Oh, let's try for this house, Theo! I could work much longer hours! I've been longing to get back to it, ever since Louis started school!'

Polly worked for a charity. Before Max and Louis, she'd travelled a lot. She was wonderful at organizing people in crisis. Wonderful. Brilliantly bossy, resourceful and kind.

'I loved it,' said Polly, 'and I'd be mostly in the offices here. It needn't be lots of travelling. A week or two perhaps, now and then.'

'OK. Listen,' said Theo. 'If I didn't run a car. No petrol bills. No parking. Cycle lanes nearly all the way to the hospital.'

'Could you really manage?' asked Polly.

'Course I could. Easy. I'd like a bike again. Pizza on the way home?'

Pizza was a celebration food. They bought it on the way back, with extra olives, mushrooms and chillis, and they parted with as many things as they could bear to let go, including Abi's signed Harry Potter and half of Max's savings, and they rented the house with the coloured glass in the windows, and the ivy and the arched front door.

CHAPTER TWO

Abi thought that now they had moved into a bigger house, they might have a pet. She mentioned it when they were in the kitchen, unpacking saucepans and china.

'A dog?' she asked. She had wanted a dog so much when she was little that she had given herself an invisible one. Roly. For two or three years, invisible Roly had slept on her bed, walked beside her to the park, shared her beanbag while she read her books. Granny Grace and Theo got used to stepping round him, and on journeys and trips out they asked now and then, 'Will Roly be coming with us?'

There had never been a real Roly, though. 'In this little flat?' Granny Grace had said. 'Not possible.'

There hadn't been a dog, there couldn't be a cat because of the traffic. There had been a hamster. A school friend had got tired of him, and Abi, despite Granny Grace's horror of small creatures like hamsters, had smuggled him home. After a good deal of fuss she had been allowed to keep him – 'But you can't hug a hamster,' said Abi, and, 'Could we have a dog or a cat?' she asked now.

Max and Louis both stopped what they were doing to listen to the answer.

'Sorry,' said Theo. 'It's a "no pets" lease. We can't have anything like that.'

'How would anyone know?'

'We're just not going to risk it,' said Theo. 'We've signed a contract that says we won't, and we've paid a thousand pounds deposit . . .'

'A THOUSAND POUNDS!' repeated Louis, stunned.

'A thousand pounds, which we can't afford to lose. That's one thing. The other is, it's only a six-month lease . . .'

'Does that mean,' demanded Max, staring around at the chaotic kitchen, 'that in six months' time we might have to shove this all back into boxes and move house again?'

'Not if the owners renew the lease,' said Polly soothingly. 'Which we are sure . . .'

'Almost sure,' said Theo.

'. . . almost sure they will. If there are no problems.'

'So, that's it, Abi,' said Theo. 'No smuggled-in surprises! We just can't take the risk.'

'No, we can't,' Max agreed. 'Don't forget my fifty pounds! Half my saved-up hundred pounds!' He glanced at Abi so distrustfully that she lost her temper.

'It's my home too!' she cried. 'This time, it's my home just as much as yours! I don't want to lose it either. And stop going on about your fifty pounds! You can get another fifty pounds, but I can't ever get another signed Harry Potter book.'

Bang! went the door as she marched out of the kitchen, and they were left with a horrible silence.

'Good for Abi!' said Polly.

'I think you should be on Max's side,' remarked Louis.

'Oh, do you?' said Polly crossly.

'Yes, 'n' Theo on Abi's side.'

'And what about you?' asked Theo.

'He can be on Mrs Puddock's side,' said Max, and Louis flew at him in fury.

Louis did not like Mrs Puddock.

It was Polly who had introduced her to the family. 'We've got a neighbour,' she said, running into the kitchen to call people. 'I found her on the path. I think she was waiting to meet us. Come and say hello to Mrs Puddock!'

'Hello, Mrs P.,' said Theo amiably. He was so tall he had to bend to look at her properly. 'Keeping an eye on us all?'

Mrs Puddock crossed little starfish hands on her stomach, and looked around at them with bright, glinting eyes. She had a nice smile, huge, stretching in a wavering, rueful line from invisible ear to invisible ear. She dipped her head a little and shuffled.

'Hello, Mrs Puddock,' said Abi, but Louis edged away.

Mrs Puddock's voice was hesitant, and a little creaky, and her movements were slow. 'She looks ancient,' said Max when they met her again, a day or two later. 'Like a dead thing come alive.'

Louis stared at him in fear.

'I'm going to make friends with her,' said Abi, causing Max to roll his eyes and Louis to beg urgently, 'Don't!'

'Why shouldn't I?'

'Because it will start Louis off on one of his stupid fusses,' said Max. 'Just leave her alone, can't you?'

Abi was not used to being told what to do, except by Granny Grace. Nor had she forgotten 'Don't forget my fifty pounds!' and Max's distrustful glance. After that she kept an extra watch out for Mrs Puddock, and met her quite often, mostly in the evenings, always close to the house. She seemed to like the shadows and the damp little path by the hedge, but the lighted windows clearly fascinated her. She would pause on her journeys to gaze.

'Do you think she notices what we do?' said Louis, and Polly said yes, of course she did, and Theo and Max should bring their bikes in properly, instead of leaving them slumped by the wall, and people should remember to take their shoes off at the door and the bins should be put out on time.

Louis looked at Polly carefully, checking that she was joking.

'Mrs Puddock,' said Theo, 'is a flipping nuisance.'

'Mrs Puddock,' said Max, 'is a really stupid joke.'

'I saw her eat a beetle,' said Louis.

'You're a good one to talk about beetles,' said Max, looking meaningfully at Louis' head, which had recently once again become home to uninvited wildlife, and he turned Louis upside down and held him by his ankles. He said he was shaking the beetles out of his hair.

'Louis' beetles are long gone,' said Theo, turning him the right way up again. 'I've checked. Right, I'm off to work. I'll see you all later. Don't drive each other nuts! Be happy.'

*

It wasn't very hard to be happy in those first weeks. It was the school summer holidays. The days were bright. Sunlight chased Mrs Puddock away, polished the ivy leaves and found its way into the rooms, dappling them with greenish light. The last boxes were unpacked, and the rooms gradually organized, the kitchen first, then the bedrooms, and then they ran out of furniture. They didn't care, because they had space. Where they had lived before they'd had so little space that everyone always knew where everyone else was to be found. Now they had room to lose track of each other.

'Cuts down on the bickering,' said Theo to Polly, and she groaned and nodded and asked, 'Will they ever get on?'

Max spent a lot of time with his friend Danny, partly because they jointly owned a bike-repair and car-cleaning business, which was based at Danny's house, and partly because Danny had taken a dislike to the ivy house the first time he'd visited.

'Spooky,' Danny had said. It was best that the bike-repair and car-cleaning business was at his house anyway, because he had four big brothers with broken bikes, as well as several kind neighbours with dirty cars. Some days the business actually earned money, or would have done if its owners hadn't immediately rushed out and spent it on bike-repair and car-cleaning equipment. They told each other this was reinvesting, but really they enjoyed spending. It made them feel optimistic. Their conversations often began with, 'When we get rich . . .'

*

Louis did not even go as far as the graveyard. He stayed at home. Those first warm nights, with his bed pushed under his window, he stretched his bare feet out into the thousand shining green leaves, and felt magic running through him like bright sap through the veins of a leaf. He had begun to know the ivy, its depth, its mysterious blue reflections, its iron smell of green and ancient botany, its sound of rain on turning pages, its strength and brittleness, and its flavour of cress and stone.

It was the first wildwood of his life, and it satisfied him all summer.

While Max was busy and Louis was studying ivy, Abi was exploring. She found a tunnel in the yew hedge, wriggled through and discovered the old graveyard. Theo wriggled after her, much to her dismay.

'Can't I have *one* private place?' she demanded.

'Yes,' said Theo, 'so long as you have it with me. I won't tell Polly and I won't tell the boys, but every time you come here, you've got to let me know.'

'Why?

'Because I'm your dad and it's my job to look out for you. Come on, Abi, promise!'

Abi promised, and so the graveyard became their secret. Over the years it had become a wild place, a patch of countryside in the middle of a city. Abi discovered hoverflies and insects amongst the long purple-headed grasses, slow-worms under the hedge, strange gold lichens painting weather-worn angels – best of all, a fox family, their cubs at dawn, light feet amongst ancient stones. Abi bought puppy biscuits and scattered them on an old table-top grave, warm in the sunshine.

MARIAN HEPPLE, 1802, AGED 9. A LOVING HEART FOR ALL GOD'S CREATURES, read the inscription.

The cubs crunched, their eyes half closed with pleasure. Abi thought Marian would be pleased. She wrote and told Granny Grace about them, and about the ivy and Mrs Puddock, and the Narnia lamp and the books she had found in her room, and the way that Polly was not as annoying as she had been at first, though Max was just as bad, and Louis even worse.

Foxes have germs, wrote back Granny Grace (ignoring Abi's grumbling as she always did):

You make sure you wash your hands. I send you a pink hibiscus flower from the bush beside my door. Tell your father that I said to be careful on his bike. Remind him that he rode into our neighbour when he was nine years old, and the dustcart when he was eleven.

Now, my very dearest Abigail, study some schoolwork so you start off well next term, and write back soon to your loving Granny Grace.

So much ivy, so much news! What a time of green magic!

Green magic, thought Abi, and nodded, because the words seemed right.

CHAPTER THREE

Towards the end of summer there was a great trying on of school uniform. Max's blazer seemed to have shrunk up his arms, and his school trousers dangled high above his bony school-socked ankles.

Louis had changed schools and needed everything new. Abi could manage, except for her shoes, but her school bag had split.

'Perhaps coats can wait for a month,' said Polly.

'Who wants coats in September?' asked Max. Louis' red sweatshirts came from his school's second-hand-uniform shop. Theo mended the split in Abi's school bag, but it still showed a bit.

Abi asked Theo privately, 'Are we paying the rent?'

'Yes we are,' said Theo, hugging her, 'and as soon as school goes back I'm picking up extra shifts. Polly's work is taking off too. In fact, there's a bit of a problem about that . . .'

The problem was that by the time the new school term began, Polly had gone from being nearly always at home, to nearly always at work. Theo seemed to be nearly always at

31

work already and, when his extra shifts began, life took a lot of organization. Polly made worry lists, adding things to the bottom faster than she ticked them off at the top. As well as school and uniform, they had had to find a school bus for Abi and a cycle route for Max.

Polly ticked *Bus Abi* and *Bike route Max* off the top of her worry list, and wrote a few more things on the bottom. The very last thing added was: *Rocking-horse room*.

The rocking-horse room was the name that first Louis, and then the whole family, had given to the sitting room.

'Do you think we'll ever get it done?' asked Polly, looking around it one day. It was still untouched, except that Rocky had moved in, together with the old sofa that was too big for the kitchen.

'It only needs cleaning, and a fire,' said Theo.

'Rugs,' said Polly, 'and curtains.'

'A proper-sized telly,' said Theo. 'Max and I are tired of miniature football.'

'Football can never be too miniature,' said Polly. 'The panelling polished and the ceiling painted.'

Theo looked up at the ceiling, which had a garland of plaster leaves and roses round the edge, all laced together with dirty cobwebs. 'Brushing first, then painting,' he said. 'That chimney needs sweeping!'

'How do you know?'

'Soot comes down when it rains. In Scotland in the old days,' said Theo, who had lived there until he was six and therefore considered himself a Scot, 'they would get a bunch of heather, tie it to a rock, climb on the roof, drop it down the chimney . . .'

'This is London,' said Polly.

'North,' said Theo. 'Practically Scotland, it's so north.'

'You can see the Shard,' said Polly. 'Sometimes. Nearly. Now and then. So it's London. Anyway, it's definitely not Scotland . . .'

She flopped down on the sofa to write 'Rocks: Chimney (No)' on her worry list.

'What else is on it?' asked Theo.

'Abi. I'm worried about Abi. She's so quiet that sometimes it's almost like she vanishes. And when she's not vanished, she's reading. Do you think she reads too much?'

'I used to wonder that, but her granny said it's not possible,' said Theo. 'And Abi and I have a vanishing agreement, so cross that off your list too. Go on, what's next?'

'Mrs Puddock.

'Mrs Puddock?'

'I knew you'd laugh, but that joke's gone on too long. Poor Louis. Oh, Theo . . .'

Theo looked at her.

'How will I tell him that I have to go away?'

'Do you, Pol?'

'Yes.'

'Not for long?'

'At least three weeks, maybe more. That's also on my list: how to tell you.'

'Polly!' said Theo, hugging her. 'We knew from the start it would probably happen. I'll look after Louis!'

'Max is on the list too. The other day he said to me, "Obviously Dad won't be coming back, now Theo's on the scene." After more than five years of not hearing a word from his father! Who knew he was thinking like that? No wonder he's sometimes so awful.'

'Max is no way anything even close to awful!' said Theo. 'You don't know what awful is, Pol! You should see some of the fourteen-year-old kids that get brought into A-and-E at two o'clock in the morning and, actually, they're not awful either.'

'I know I should worry about all the other fourteen-year-olds in London,' said Polly, 'but right now I just care about Max. He's not got his head round you and Abi yet, and now there's Esmé . . .'

'Max will soon get used to Esmé,' said Theo.

'Esmé' was Esmé-the-Art-Student. She was the latest addition to the house. Her job was to pick Louis up from his After-school Club and stay with him until a grown-up got home. Neither Max nor Abi could do it, because picker-uppers had to be over sixteen. Until Theo's shifts changed, after Christmas, Esmé was the only way to save Louis from a ten-hour-long school day.

Polly had found her by way of a friend who worked at the art college. The friend was Danny's mum. That was the problem.

'*Why* did you have to ask Danny's mum to find someone for Louis?' demanded Max, crashing into the kitchen the first day he heard the news.

'Why not? She works at the art college – she's the perfect person!' said Polly. 'She was bound to know a student who wanted to earn a bit extra by . . .'

'. . . babysitting!' Max had finished, dropping his school bag and kicking it. 'Babysitting!' he repeated, slumping down in a kitchen chair. 'Babysitting!' he complained, shoving away a mug of tea so hard it tipped and flooded the table, Louis' homework book and a pile of clean school shirts.

'Max!'

'Leave me alone!' said Max.

The school week had started perfectly well for Max – very well, hilariously well – only the day before. He'd arrived in the entrance hall just in time see his good friend Danny doing his morning locker-jumps. Danny was as short as Max was tall. He was the shortest person in the school. Yet at the start of term he'd been given a top-row locker. Out of pride, he'd refused to swap. Instead, he did a lot of jumping.

So far, Max had politely ignored his friend's locker-jumping antics. He should have carried on ignoring them. He should not have laughed and gripped him by the shoulders of his next-eldest brother's old, ripped parka and hoisted him up to reach.

And yet, at the time, Max had hardly noticed he had done

it. It had just been a five-minute joke, the sort of thing he did to Louis every day.

However, Danny wasn't Louis. Louis didn't care. Danny did.

Danny had spluttered and wriggled until he tumbled right to the floor, leaving his empty jacket in Max's hands. Then he had scrambled to his feet, grabbed his jacket and marched away without a word.

His revenge had come the next morning.

That day, Danny, trusted partner in the bike-repair and car-cleaning business – long-time-best-friend Danny – had yelled across the crowded school entrance hall, 'Oi, Max! My mum says she's found you a really good babysitter!'

'What?' Max demanded. 'What did you just say? What?'

'She's found you a babysitter!' Danny had shouted, even louder than the first time. 'She said to tell you to let your mum know. Esmé, she's called! She's an art student . . .'

Danny had to pause at that point to double up with laughter at the sight of Max's face. 'She can be with you every day, right up to Christmas . . .'

'What are you actually on about, Danny?'

'She's just what you need, Mum said. And she's French.'

'French? French? What d'you mean, French?'

'French is what they call people from France,' explained Danny (now enjoying himself very much indeed). 'E.g. your new babysitter. Don't tell me you don't want a French babysitter, Max!'

Lots of people were listening now, listening and laughing

and egging Danny on. People coming in late were asking, 'Hey! What's this about?'

'It's about Esmé-the-Art-Student,' Danny explained obligingly. 'My mum's sorted her out for Max. To babysit. She's French!'

Howls of laughter, calls and whistles.

'I've got a picture if you want to see what she's like,' continued Danny helpfully. 'From when I went in to college with Mum yesterday to help set up an exhibition. There!'

Danny fished out his phone and produced a photo of his mum's art class, with himself in the middle, like a mascot.

Max had refused to look, but everyone else crowded round. 'Wow!' said some of the boys, and, 'Definitely French!' said some of the girls.

'Too good for Maxi-babe, that's for sure!' said awful Danny, ex-best friend.

Max's French babysitter was the best news of the term.

Ever since then, Max – round-faced, logical, ordinary Max, the Max who had made the first joke, and was even almost beginning to get his head round Theo and Abi – had become a new person. A bad-tempered, door-slamming, prejudiced-against-art-students type of person. A person who found it completely impossible to be in the same room as eighteen-year-old Esmé, preferring, if necessary, to sulk upstairs for hours.

Whatever Theo said to comfort Polly, Max had not got used to Esmé.

A few weeks after Esmé started looking after Louis, Polly went away. She stuffed the freezer, picked an ivy leaf or two for company on the journey, hugged them all, said, 'Look after each other! Don't forget to sort the recycling!' and vanished.

Suddenly the house was different. Max, who had laughed at Danny's 'spooky' in the summer, now wondered: *Is it?*

One day they'd had a power cut at school, and everyone had been sent home early. Max had arrived at an empty house and, looking up at Louis' window, glimpsed a swift movement.

Max was no coward. He'd unlocked the front door, clattered his bike into the dark hall, propped it against the wall, and gone straight up to Louis' room. There was Louis' tidy bed pushed under the window and his row of cardboard boxes lined up against the wall, his chest of drawers, with a neat line of small cars, and another of ivy leaves, his shelf of stuff: the unhugged teddy bear and the unopened boxes of Lego from his last birthday, the unpulled Christmas crackers and the intact Easter egg.

Everything immobile. Not a flicker of movement.

CRASH! went Max's bike downstairs in the hall, and Max turned and raced downstairs.

There was no one there either.

Spooky? wondered Max.

Abi also felt the change. Theo was working. Polly was gone, and Abi was surprised how much she missed her. At first she'd thought (feeling guilty), *One person less to share Dad*, but it didn't seem to work like that. No Polly made Theo extra busy, and Louis extra demanding of attention. Esmé wasn't enough for him. She brought her art work back with her, and when it was spread out on the kitchen table, she became entirely absorbed. Often, when Louis bothered her with questions, she answered him in French. 'You're in London!' Louis would protest, and Esmé would murmur, '*Mais oui.*'

Max made everything more uncomfortable. He stayed in his bedroom, refusing to admit that Esmé existed. His silent resentment of her seeped under his bedroom door, and down the stairs, and added a shadow to the days.

The fox cubs were grown and scattered, and the evenings cold and dark. Abi would have been lonely, except she had books. Books, and also the house. Abi never thought, *Spooky*, because she loved it. The glow of the Narnia lamp. The warmth of wood under her hand. The friendly creak of the stairs. Her own private room. And the feeling of living in a guarded space, cloaked in green ivy leaves. She told Granny Grace, 'This house is kind.'

My sweet Abigail, Granny Grace wrote back. *I am so happy your house is kind . . .*

Granny Grace could email and Skype, and she did, now and then, but more often she wrote letters on thin blue paper, usually with a flower or two folded amongst the pages. Proper letters that arrived through the letter box, and could be carried around all day, with detailed instructions for the best (and only) way for Abi to manage her life.

While you have the French girl with you, take your chance and learn the language, wrote Granny Grace. *You will find it comes easily; there are many French words in English. Make sure you get your sleep and your bones will grow strong and long . . .*

Louis envied those letters.

'Abi, couldn't Granny Grace write to me?' he begged.

'No!' exclaimed Abi. (Was she going to have to share Granny Grace now, as well as everything else?) 'Anyway, why? You hate reading!'

Louis didn't argue. It was true. He wouldn't read and he didn't read. He detested it. Loathed the little black words that crawled like beetles across the pages. Hated the way that as soon as he had laboured through one boring paper-covered book, he was handed another, even harder.

Still, he longed for a letter of his own.

'Granny Grace could send me a flower, like yours,' he suggested. 'No writing, just a flower – couldn't she?'

'No.'

Louis gave a great sniff and wiped his nose on his hand. He'd caught a cold. No matter how quickly people passed him tissues, they were never quite in time. He sneezed unconfined sneezes. Abi searched the kitchen cupboards and made him a hot lemony drink with honey in it.

'I might not like it,' he said.

'Doesn't matter, you still have to drink it.'

'Can I ride Rocky if I do?'

'No. Not till your nose has stopped running.'

'What if it never stops?'

'Then you never can. Get on with your lemon. Breathe the steam!'

'Why?' asked Louis.

'Granny Grace always says that.'

'Tell me some more about her,' said Louis, breathing steam so industriously that Abi found herself sharing a little piece of Granny Grace after all.

'She used to bake cakes on Saturday mornings. I used to help.'

'What sort of cakes?'

'All sorts. Chocolate. Orange and lemon. Toto cake like she had when she was little in Jamaica.'

'What's Toto cake?'

'Coconut with lime and spices. Cinnamon and nutmeg.' Even to name those spices gave Abi a pang of wistfulness for Granny Grace and her spice cupboard, and the smell of toasted coconut, and the small sunny kitchen with its windowsill filled with growing plants.

'She grew ginger root in a flowerpot. We used to wait for it to flower.'

'Did it?'

'Yes.'

'Could we grow it?'

'I suppose.'

'And make that cake with coconut?'

'Not until you stop sneezing everywhere.'

'Oh,' said Louis, sniffing hideously. 'What else?'

'She would make you do your homework,' said Abi, sternly. 'Where's your reading book?'

'It wasn't reading homework today,' lied Louis. 'Homework today was colouring in.'

'Well, go and do it!'

Louis sighed, but settled down at the kitchen table with his pencils. Esmé was already there, engrossed as usual. She had spread out her huge, heavy portfolio book. It was full of drawings and paintings, with glued-in scrapbook samples, unfolding maps, and colour patches: yellow ochre, rust red, charcoal dark. It fascinated Louis.

Abi, busy with her own homework in the rocking-horse room, where she could guard Rocky while she worked, heard Louis ask, 'Can I help, Esmé?'

And Esmé's firm reply: '*Non.*'

It became peaceful. Abi finished her maths, and picked up the old hardback book with the blue cover from the collection she had found in her bedroom. It was the one that had the seashell ocean sound, and the strange words in the title: *Kon-Tiki.*

The parrot fidgeted, high up on the crossbeam over the dark square sail, the long blue waves lifted and rolled, slapping against the raft. Reflected light glinted and scattered, the sun was high overhead.

'*We were visited by whales many times. Most often they were small porpoises . . .*'

The parrot left its perch to fly, grass-green wings, coral-red beak, dark primary feathers spread like a fan against the sun-bleached sky . . .

'Abi, Abi, Abi! Abi, I can't see you!'

'Here, on the sofa,' said Abi, blinking, half dazzled by Pacific sunlight.

'There was . . .'

'What?'

But Louis had forgotten.

It was easy to forget, to close the blue covers and lose the unbelievable. Abi did it every time, so completely that she was startled in the kitchen when Louis looked at her book and asked, 'Why is it all wet?'

'What?'

'Your book. Look.'

It *was* all wet, dark with water, and the pages buckled with damp.

'I don't know . . .' she began, puzzled, and then remembered, in the way that dreams are remembered, in fragments and fading images, sunlight, a blue ocean and a blue circle of horizon. The way she had slipped.

The ocean sound, like the echo in a seashell. Her stinging eyes.

Cautiously she touched the stained cover, and once again tasted her fingertip.

Salt.

She checked again.

Definitely salt.

CHAPTER FOUR

Louis had a secret, and it had started with owls. 'Owls': a word so short and open that he could not quite hear it. *'Nowls'*, thought Louis, *is better.*

Louis had started changing words when he was little, three or four years old, with grommets in his ears. At that time he had struggled to hear not only the things other people said, but also those he said himself, and he had got into a way of making words a bit more audible by adding an extra letter or two. He had nearly grown out of it, but there were still one or two words left. There were *nowls,* and there was *iffen*, which was 'if'.

Iffen there's a nowl, thought Louis. Ever since he had first heard of Harry Potter, he had longed for nowls. Regularly he had explained to his family his need for one. They had been absolutely useless. They had bought him a toy: a furry Hedwig in a plastic cage. They said a real nowl was impossible.

That was before the new ivy-covered house.

Possible now, thought Louis. Had he not heard them calling, that very first-time night? *Wild nowls*, thought Louis, up in his bare, immaculate room: bed, chest of drawers, a rug made out of nine carpet square samples taped together underneath, dark floorboards.

A good room, like an ivy-wrapped den. A perfect place for a nowl, if only a nowl would come.

They could make nests in the ivy, thought Louis. *There's plenty of room.*

It was true that the ivy was tremendous around Louis' window. It hung in bunches from knotted twisty stems as thick as his arm: a deep, green, vertical forest. Really it was surprising that it wasn't already full of nowls.

Perhaps they just haven't noticed it yet, thought Louis.

How, how, how, he wondered, to make a nowl find his ivy? That was the problem.

Then there came a day when Louis discovered a dead mouse on the path by the door.

Louis pocketed the mouse, and later he put it on his windowsill and waited.

The mouse disappeared.

Louis was not so fortunate as to find a supply of dead mice, but he used his brains and thought of other things that might tempt a hungry nowl. Ham from his friends' packed-lunch sandwiches. A discarded chicken kebab found in the street. Would a nowl eat cheese? It seemed it would; cheese vanished in the night, and so did scrambled eggs. Veggie sausages were rejected, though, and so were mushrooms. Crisps were pecked at, but then scattered through the ivy. Louis never caught his nowl in action; it waited till he was asleep.

Then came the day when he and Theo found the pigeon.

It was just after Polly went away.

Theo said the pigeon must have been hit by a car. He was with Louis when they came across it, motionless, in front of the house, its feathers ruffled, its head limp and sad, its eyes asleep.

'Don't touch it,' said Theo, his arm round Louis' shoulders, his deep voice as warm as sunlight. 'And don't cry. One bump, and all over. It wouldn't have known.'

'It might wake up,' said Louis, but Theo shook his head, and said, 'Don't think so, old Louis, leave it alone now, and we'll do a funeral after tea.' Then Theo had taken off his beanie hat, wrapped it gently round the pigeon, and moved it into the shade of the house. They had gone inside and Louis had become quite springy and cheerful, but a couple of hours later, when Theo went out again, he said, 'Well. That's funny.'

Because there was only the hat.

Theo didn't say anything else because he thought Louis must have forgotten the pigeon. Louis didn't say anything either because it was now upstairs, reviving (he hoped) in a specially made nest in the ivy.

The pigeon was still asleep when Louis went to bed, but it looked much better, dozing in its nest, with its feathers properly smooth and its sleepy head resting on a leaf. Louis patted it with satisfaction, spread pepperoni slices all along the windowsill, and went to sleep himself.

That was the first night that Louis saw his visitor. A silhouette against the night sky, a Russian doll, with ears.

Ears? thought Louis, and in the morning he drew what he had seen and showed it to Abi.

'Guess what?' said Louis.

'An owl,' said Abi.

'Yes, a nowl,' agreed Louis. 'With ears.'

Abi nodded. She didn't say, 'Owls can't have ears,' so Louis knew they could.

Wonderfully, the pigeon had revived and flown away in the night, two small feathers left in payment to Louis for his kindness. Louis pushed the feathers behind his ears to help his magic, and renewed his offerings on the windowsill. He longed for another glimpse. 'Nowl, come back. Come back, nowl,' he murmured as he fell asleep.

Then one night (stolen school fish fingers on the windowsill) it happened, and he saw.

His nowl was brown. A blotched sort of brown. It *did* have ears, and it was large.

The faintest shadow of doubt began in Louis' mind. The songs that he droned when he was all alone changed a little. 'Iffen you're a nowl?' he sang. And sometimes, 'What iffen . . . what iffen, what iffen you're not?'

The magic of the nowl made up a little for the missing-ness of Polly.

Polly called them almost every evening; they put her on speakerphone so everyone could hear. She had a way of talking as if she were in a room next door.

'Pop upstairs, Abi, and look in the airing cupboard. That

shampoo you wanted is somewhere on the right. I meant to give it to you. What on earth is that noise on the stairs?'

'Just Max coming down on his bike.'

'Max!'

'Where else round here can I practise mountain biking?' asked Max. 'Anyway, I've stopped, the chain's come off again.'

'It probably needs tightening – get Theo to help you. Has Louis done his reading homework yet?'

Theo said no he hadn't, and what about if Louis read to Polly, right now?

'But first blow your nose, Louis,' called Polly, 'because sniffing and reading at the same time is very difficult . . . What was that? Where's he gone? Louis?'

They found Louis in bed, unwashed but snoring. He refused to wake up.

'We know you're pretending,' said Abi sternly.

'Come on, Louis,' said Theo. 'I've brought the phone. Sit up and say bye to your mum.'

'Goodnight, Louis, you sleep well,' called Polly. 'I love you. I'll see you soon.'

'When?' said Louis, eyes still shut but talking in his sleep, since the reading danger seemed over. 'P'raps tomorrow?'

'Well, not tomorrow.'

'The next day?'

'Maybe a little longer.'

'I don't want a little longer,' said Louis woefully. 'What about Christmas?'

'I'll be back ages before Christmas!' said Polly, thousands

of miles away. 'Gosh, yes, ages! What do you want for Christmas?'

'A nowl,' said Louis, 'I told you.'

'Louis, please think of something else,' said Polly briskly. 'Because no one can possibly get you an owl . . . and don't start that snoring again!'

But Louis did start the snoring, and this time it was unstoppable. One by one, his family gave up and left him, and when they had gone he opened wide his window, despite the autumn chill. Then he laid an offering of cold marmite toast on the windowsill and whispered, 'Are you there . . . ?'

What did he hope for? Unfurling brown wings and a drifting warmth? Wise round eyes to watch while he slept? He awoke to find a warm living shape pressing him into his mattress.

This was so terrifying that for several hours (or so it seemed) Louis stopped breathing. Nor did he open his eyes. But he did not have to look to know that no owl, no nowl, nor anything that flew in the sky, was such a tremendous weight.

Sometime after midnight, whatever-it-was shifted. Whatever-it-was raised itself and began kneading Louis under the quilt. It seemed very strong and it had claws. Every now and then, Louis heard a thread rip when they caught. Once, when that happened, something lashed: *whump, whump!*

Louis unscrewed his eyes and, in the dim light, he saw a long, furry tail.

He clutched his quilt and squeaked.

Whatever-it-was growled, so low in its throat, that the vibrations ran through the bed like electric pulses, but the sound soon died away.

Louis collected his courage. There was a bedside lamp on top of his chest of drawers. He stretched out a cautious arm and switched it on.

Then Louis looked and looked and looked at his golden-eyed, hot-furred, heavy-pawed conjuring from out of the ivy-rustling night.

And the conjuring looked at him.

'You climbed up the ivy,' whispered Louis.

It did not deny it.

'You're not a nowl,' said Louis. 'I guessed you weren't, when I saw your ears. And now you've got fur. You're a cat,' said Louis, but he spoke uncertainly. *Was* this a cat? 'A cat-thing,' said Louis.

The cat-thing sank down, deep and heavy on the bed. The night air from the window was cold, but the cat-thing was warm. Louis found himself wishing it would purr.

'Iffen . . .' he murmured, and found the cat-thing's eyes on his, a direct golden gaze that went straight to his astonished, worshipping soul. 'Iffen . . .' he said again, and the cat-thing dipped its golden head in acknowledgement.

So then Louis knew that was its name.

Iffen.

CHAPTER FIVE

For a day or two after the evening that Abi had slipped and dropped her book through time and space and logic and into the South Pacific, she stopped reading. She left *The Kon-Tiki Expedition* in the rocking-horse room and closed the door. She tried not to think of how the raft had swung over the waves, and how her hair had caught the sea spray. She told herself, *It was a dream. You were falling asleep.*

Yes, but the book was wet, argued Abi with Abi.

Perhaps, before you were quite awake, you dropped it in a puddle.

What puddle?

A puddle of rain that had blown in earlier when somebody opened the window.

Salt rain?

But Abi pushed away the thought of salt.

Don't forget the sound! said persistent, arguing Abi. *The seashell ocean sound! And don't say perhaps it was just wind in the chimney!*

*

But perhaps it *was* wind in the chimney, thought Abi, a few days later, up in her bedroom, finishing homework. Outside, a gusty autumn breeze was rattling the ivy leaves. Might the wind blowing over the chimney make a sound like an ocean's rolling waves? Abi thought she might go down to the rocking-horse room and listen.

It was one of the rare days when Theo was home early. He was in the bathroom with Louis. They had filled the bath to its maximum depth and Louis was having deep-sea-diving lessons while Theo simultaneously cleaned the bathroom, sorted laundry, and trimmed his own hair because he didn't have time to go to a barber. As Abi passed the door, she heard a burst of laughter and paused.

'Can't see a thing in this mirror!' she heard Theo complain. 'All steamed up! Which side needs a bit more, left or right?'

Then Louis' voice – Louis, who didn't know left from right – calling, 'That one! That one, that one by your ear . . . Not that ear, the other ear!'

Then more laughter.

Abi felt a lurch of sour green jealousy. It was the hair-cutting game that she and her father had played when she was little. It was a part of her childhood. The same jokes ('*Whoooops!*'), the same pretend-anxious vanity: 'Am I looking good yet, Louis?' Worst of all, snatches of a song that had been hers and Theo's ever since she could first remember.

My song! thought Abi (with no idea of how many children in A&E had been triaged, bathed, stitched, bandaged, held

54

over sick bowls, wheeled down corridors, comforted in their fear to snatches of that same familiar tune).

Once, long before Abi could remember, there had been her mother and father and herself. Three of them, with Abi safe in the warm heart of the family. But that had been broken.

Then there had been Granny Grace, who for ten bossy, loving years had left Abi in no doubt that her only grandchild was the centre of her world. Until Granny Grace rushed off to Jamaica.

Now it seemed Theo could manage without her, too. It was all Abi could do not to barge into the bathroom, spoil the fun, wail loudly, 'Find a new game for Louis! A new game and a new song! That one's mine!'

But she didn't. She heroically carried on downstairs, and she arrived at the closed door of the rocking-horse room.

The wind was blowing in the chimney, a gusty, dusty, woodwind sound. Not a bit like the ocean.

But still Abi could hear splashing and laughter from the bathroom, and still she remembered the taste of salt.

I know why people run away, thought Abi bitterly, but since she didn't have anywhere to run to, she opened the door of the rocking-horse room instead. There was the book, exactly where she'd left it, and suddenly it was as tempting as an unopened parcel, a shooting star not wished on, a chance not taken. However, when she picked it up she found that it would not open; the pages were stuck together. In that cold, empty room, the book had stayed as damp as when she'd left it.

'It's *not fair!*' exclaimed Abi, about everything in the world, and she stamped into the kitchen, put her book into the microwave, turned the setting to 'Auto Roast High' and pressed START.

The results were immediate. The silver lettering fragmented into crackling golden sparks and there was a hot, fishy smell. For a horrible few seconds Abi feared she had microwaved an ocean. It did have the good effect of making Max, who had his bike upside down in the corner, trying to fix the chain, look up and speak.

'What the heck are you doing?' he demanded.

'I was trying to dry my book,' said Abi, opening the window wide and wafting a tea towel about. 'Why does it smell of fish?'

'It's the glue,' said Max. 'They made glue out of fishbones and horses' hooves and all sorts of disgusting stuff in the olden days. Microwaves are rubbish for drying things anyway. I tried it with my trainers once. I didn't know the bits round the lace holes were metal.'

'What happened?' asked Abi, brightening a bit because this was the friendliest that Max had been for weeks.

'They made blue lightning and then they caught fire,' said Max. 'What's the book about?'

'A raft.'

'Go on.'

Abi tried, although talking much still didn't come easily, especially talking to Max. 'Ages ago, these people built a raft out of logs and set out to see if they could sail across the Pacific Ocean. They had a parrot, and there were flying fish.'

'Great,' said Max, sounding like he wished he hadn't asked.

'I skipped a lot at the beginning.'

'I would have too,' said Max.

'There's a picture of it.' Abi carefully unpeeled the still-damp pages to find the photographs at the back. 'Those logs were really slippery. If you stepped on the wrong place like I . . .'

Abi stopped.

'What?'

'Nothing,' said Abi, not wanting Max to think she was insane. 'Why is my dad bathing Louis?'

'Someone's got to,' said Max.

'I mean now, so early.'

'I s'pose to cheer him up.'

'What was the matter?'

'I had an atlas out that I brought back from school. Louis saw it and started trying to work out where Mum was.'

'Does he understand maps?'

'No. Well, he didn't at first. I showed him where she was and it didn't mean a thing to him. He was pleased. He said, 'Oh, that's not far. Can we go?' So, to make him understand how far it was, I showed him Scotland, because of going there that time when we all went on their honeymoon . . .'

'I hated that,' said Abi.

'It was seriously weird,' agreed Max. 'Anyway, I shouldn't have bothered because when Louis got that Mum was about ten times as far away as Scotland he started wailing and he didn't stop until your dad came in and said, "What about a deep-sea-diving lesson? I've got time if you have," and took him upstairs.'

'I think he's all right now,' said Abi. 'He sounded fine when I went past.'

'Till the next time,' said Max.

The next time came minutes later, with another call from Polly. Louis and Theo came racing down the stairs, both very damp, and Polly began her usual rapid-fire questions about clean school uniform, what they'd had for supper, if Louis had forgotten to worry about Mrs Puddock yet and whether Theo was remembering to pay Esmé.

'Polly,' said Theo reproachfully.

'OK, I'm sorry,' said Polly. 'Is Louis there? I didn't get to talk to him last time.'

'I poked my reading book,' said Louis, grabbing the phone to himself and speaking in a very loud voice, 'down a DRAIN.'

'Louis!'

'Where you are, are there BOMBS?'

'Louis, of course n—'

'Have you got a GUN?' asked Louis, dodging Max and Theo, now both trying to grab the phone from him.

'Absolutely not!'

'What about STABBERS?'

'What, Louis? What?'

'Stabbers with KNIVES,' said Louis, now under the kitchen table with his back against the wall and practically unreachable. 'I've seen the news on telly! I've seen ALL the news! Who would win a fight, you or a STABBER?'

'Louis, please could you put Theo on for a minute, and after that I'll talk to you again.'

'Muuuuuumm!' howled Louis, and flung the phone away from him. It went skittering across the kitchen tiles and Theo stopped it with his foot and scooped it up and said, 'Sorry about that, Pol. Overtired . . . Bedtime any minute . . . Call you back soon.'

He put down the phone and, lifting aside the table as cheerfully as if he hadn't just worked a ten-hour shift, cycled three miles and gone straight into deep-sea-diving lessons, said, 'Now, hot choc all round. Come on, Abi! Can you get that started? Louis-dude, how'd you like to sleep with me tonight?'

'Yuck,' said Louis.

'Fair enough. Well then, what if I camp on your floor?'

'No,' said Louis.

'Shall I read you a storybook down here, then, while Abi makes the choc? I used to read to Abi – didn't I, Abi – before she learned to do it herself.'

'It's *why* I learned to do it myself,' said Abi.

'I haven't any storybooks,' said Louis sulkily.

'Yeah, we need to talk about that,' said Theo. 'That reading-book-down-the-drain thing. Not now, though. Abi, you'll have books somewhere?'

'Not that would do for Louis. We gave them all away to the hospital.'

'Max?'

Max went to search his room and came down with his school English book, which was about a murdered boy called Piggy, and a bright red paperback labelled *Worst Case Scenario*.

'No, no, no, no!' said Theo, tucking Louis into a corner of the kitchen armchair, and settling down beside him. 'Last thing we need right now! It'll have to be a story out my head, then.'

Abi groaned.

'Once upon a time . . .'

'You're so rubbish at this it's embarrassing,' said Abi, splashing hot chocolate into mugs.

'There were these three bears,' continued Theo, undaunted, reaching for a mug for Louis and another for himself, 'and these bears loved porridge and so they made a big pot of it, like you do . . .'

Theo covered a yawn and said, 'Excuse me, it's sitting down sends me sleepy. Drink your choc, Lou. These bears. Yes. And their porridge. Yes. Well, it was so hot they couldn't touch it, not like this hot chocolate, which is hardly hot at all, Abi. So anyway, the bears huffed and puffed . . .'

'It was a wolf huffed and puffed, not bears,' said Abi.

'. . . the bears huffed and puffed, like wolves they huffed and puffed, and they said, "Darn this porridge, we'll leave it to cool a little," and they went back to bed.'

'No they didn't,' said Louis. 'They went for a walk.'

'OK, they went for a walk in the . . . in the jungle. They

were looking for some ice, to cool that porridge . . . You sleepy yet, Louis?'

'No,' said Louis, gulping his chocolate.

'Walking in the jungle, looking for ice, and of course they got lost, and who should they meet but a big bad . . . no they didn't, wrong story . . . a little girl in a red cloak . . . no, not her, another little girl . . . Help me out here, Abi? Max?'

'I think they met a woodcutter with a gun,' said Max.

'They didn't meet anyone!' said Abi.

'They did,' said Theo, yawning again. 'There's definitely a girl in this bear story. I'm one hundred per cent sure that there is. Later she does a lot of damage. Not the red cloak girl, another one . . . Give me a minute, and I'll be there . . .'

Just in time, Abi caught his mug as his head dropped forward. He was asleep, and Louis, snug in his corner, his fears for Polly forgotten, his head against Theo's arm, was also asleep.

'Don't you worry . . .' murmured Theo, and this time Abi hardly felt a pang of jealousy. Instead she made *Shush!* signs to Max, who nodded and picked up his *Worst Case* book. Abi wished she had a book too, but the only one within her reach was *The Kon-Tiki Expedition*, and this did not seem to be a good time to be plunged into the Pacific Ocean.

Idly, she watched Max, flicking through worst-case illustrations, and her mind flickered with the turning pages until a particular picture caught her attention.

It was a picture of a bus balanced half over a cliff. The bus's door was at the front, and open into space.

There was something about that scene. It was just a

black-and-white sketch and yet it made Abi's heart race. *Awful*, she thought, and her mind filled with questions. What would you do? If you saw it? If you were in it? Would you crawl to the back? Would it rock as you inched along the dusty, grubby aisle between the seats? Could you break the back window – but you'd have to climb up to reach . . . ? How could you break it, anyway?

Oh, thank goodness, a fire safety hammer behind a round screen!

In Case of Emergency, Abi read.

This was surely an emergency.

Abi reached upwards, but it was a huge mistake. The bus moved, moved again, lurched, and she gasped.

'Abi?' demanded Max. 'Abi? You OK?'

Louis half woke, but pushed his head deeper against Theo's arm and carried on dreaming. Theo dragged himself into wakefulness to ask, 'What? What?'

'Nothing,' said Abi, but her heart was pounding. She looked at Max, who had already lost interest and turned the page. Her thoughts were skittering like fallen leaves in the wind. *Not just the raft book! Another book now!*

Her hands felt strange, gritty and dusty from the floor of the bus. When she tiptoed up to the bathroom to wash them, the water ran grey. Back in the quiet kitchen a new realization came to her.

Not just words, but pictures.

'Bed,' mumbled Theo, and stretched, observed Louis fast asleep, and gathered them both into uprightness in one huge movement. 'Bed,' he repeated, with Louis dangled limply over his shoulder. 'Get the door for me, please, will you, Abi?'

Abi opened the kitchen door, followed him up the first set of stairs, and watched as Louis was set down, tucked into bed, photographed on Theo's phone and sent to Polly under the heading '*All wonderful*'. He stirred as they turned to go and commanded blurrily, 'Openawind . . .'

'Too cold,' said Theo.

'I WANT . . .' began Louis, showing signs of waking up far too much, like milk in a saucepan suddenly boiling.

'OK, OK,' said Theo hastily.

Wind breathed through ivy. A green coolness came rustling into the room. Louis subsided. 'Iffen . . .' he whispered, like a secret word from a private spell, and then, quite suddenly, snug as an owl in its feathers, fell asleep.

Outside the door Theo and Abi looked at each other.

'Peace,' said Theo. 'When little kids finally pack in fighting it and sleep . . . You think they never will and then it's like they flip a switch . . .'

Once again, he yawned immensely.

'. . . Sometimes, Abi, you just have to believe in magic.'

Abi thought of the seashell echo of the ocean, the startling lurch of the bus on the cliff, the wind through the ivy, Louis' last whispered word.

'Yes,' she agreed, 'you do.'

Chapter Six

I ffen did not tolerate closed windows. Louis had already discovered that. There had been a night when he jumped awake at the thud of a heavy blow, right by his head.

Thwack!

A paw: five black cat pads pressed imperiously against the glass. A husky yowl. The sound of something threshing backwards and forwards in the ivy: Iffen's tail, lashing with fury.

'Wait! Wait!' begged Louis.

The pungent smell of crushed leaves poured in the moment Louis scrabbled open the window. Iffen stalked amongst it, an outraged emperor with a cloak of green scent billowing around him. Every part of him, from his carved golden profile to his blunt, black-tipped tail, commanded, 'Don't ever do that again!'

'But,' Louis had asked, scrunching up his knees to leave Iffen the best part of the bed, 'what if it's raining?'

'What if it is?' replied a flicker of muscle in Iffen's shoulder. 'Snow?'

Iffen looked contemptuously down his nose.

'I love you,' Louis had offered hopefully, and Iffen, after a moment or two of thinking about this, had allowed his body to fold into warmth at Louis' feet.

Ever since, Louis had slept with his window open, hoping that Iffen would come back. On the night of the deep-sea-diving, and the terrible phone call and the Three Bears, it happened. Louis woke to the smell of green magic filling the room and a lovely warmth, comforting his knees.

'Iffen,' he murmured thankfully, and then as he woke up further, 'Iffen, my mum . . .'

The warmth increased.

'. . . Why does she talk in a happy voice? Why doesn't she be sad, likes she wants to come home?'

Iffen looked entirely unconcerned.

'She likes it there, that's why,' said Louis. 'She likes it there *too much*!'

He kicked in frustration. Iffen turned his head to contemplate him, and his eyes were not friendly.

'Sorry,' said Louis.

The grey-gold head turned away.

'There's only Theo now. And he's always busy. Busy at the hospital. Busy at home. And he thinks Mrs Puddock is funny.'

Louis paused for a long time, thinking about Mrs Puddock. 'Abi likes her,' he said sombrely.

Iffen, appearing bored, lowered his head and closed his eyes. Louis nevertheless continued his list of grumbles.

'Max is cross all the time. There's Esmé, but . . .'

Iffen's ears twitched.

'She's *small*. What's the use of that? If there was stabbers or kidnappers, Esmé couldn't fight them.'

Iffen yawned, clearly not very much disturbed to hear all this. He flexed a pawful of thorny black claws, considered them for a moment, and then slumped on to his side. Louis became quiet, because there was nothing else to say. Presently he scriggled down in bed until he and Iffen were back to back, with the covers between them.

'Never go away, Iffen,' he murmured as the knots of tension between his shoulders began to loosen, the clamped coldness in his stomach relaxed and the stiffness left his curled fingers and elbows and knees. 'Never go away, please, never go away, but . . .'

Louis sat up suddenly, jerking Iffen outrageously.

'. . . don't let anyone see you! I forgot! They said no pets!'

Then Iffen gave him such a glance, such a deep, long glance, that all Louis' thoughts trembled and scattered and rearranged themselves in new patterns, like a kaleidoscope shaken. Iffen a pet? Iffen was no pet. He was . . . What was he?

Louis' mind rifled his memory for all the words that might describe Iffen: 'guest', 'beast', 'cat', 'angel', 'fear', 'secret', 'wildness'.

A wildness.

Yes.

When the right word came, Louis settled down again, with Iffen heavy beside him, and this time he slept till morning.

Chapter Seven

M ax and Danny's quarrel did not fade back to normality. It got worse. Max was superb at holding grudges. Danny could never let a good joke go.

Nor a bad joke, either.

'How's the babysitter?' he asked, one Friday morning. 'Does she help with your buttons? Does she make you tidy your toys?'

Danny, who loved an audience, always found well-crowded places for these questions.

'Does she cut your food up for you? Does she read you a story before she puts you to bed?'

'Sorry, Daniel Clarence Ambrose,' replied Max. 'What did you just say?'

'Don't call me that!' snarled Danny, beaten for the moment at least.

'Why not?' asked Max politely. 'Those are your names, aren't they? Don't you remember telling me about how it was after your grandads: Clarence after the one that was called Clarence, Ambrose after the one that was called Ambrose . . .'

'Who's called Ambrose?' asked someone, overhearing. 'What kind of a name is Ambrose? Weird!'

'It's a sort of custard my gran buys in a tin,' said a blonde girl helpfully.

'Danny Clarence Custard,' said Max thoughtfully.

'Maxi-babe, stick your dummy back in!' snapped Danny.

They were both relieved when the bell went.

Max went home wondering if he could possibly change schools. No, he realized, almost at once, not after they'd bought him all that new uniform. Danny would never leave either; Danny liked school so much he was glad when the holidays ended. Nor would either of them ever be expelled, because no one ever was at their school. They just kept being nice to you until you broke down. It was going to be like this until they were both eighteen . . .

Ping! went his mobile phone, just as he arrived home, and it was Danny and it seemed that they were continuing the battle by text now. Max paused by the Narnia lamp and read:

You've nicked my bike pump. I know it was you.

You owe me £4.49, Max typed from the doorstep. Pay up, you crook.

His reply took a while to go. His and Danny's texts rarely flew swiftly, as messages should. Quite often they arrived late, or fragmented, or in flocks, all at once. He and Danny both had technology problems. Danny's was his unreliable phone (worn-out battery, cracked screen, gaffer-taped across the back, passed on from any number of elder brothers, the only iPhone 4 in the school). Max's primitive Nokia was still intact and so tough you could drop it on concrete and although it would split into three parts on impact, these could be clipped together again like Lego and it would work just the same. But perhaps it had been dropped too often. Max frequently found himself waving it in the air to get a signal, and at home it was particularly bad, and got worse and worse the further a person went into the house, until by the time it reached the attic bedrooms it was hardly there at all. Max thought it was the ivy, but Abi, who had also noticed it, said it was the house.

Louis had agreed, saying, 'Mobile phones are the wrong sort of magic.'

'Mobiles aren't magic,' Max had told him scornfully.

'How do they work, then?' asked Louis, surprised, and that shut Max up because he hadn't the faintest idea how they worked.

Probably magic.

His was pinging again.

Your cheesy trainers that you left at mine are in the bin, wrote Danny

WHAT, MY NIKES? demanded Max from halfway up to his bedroom, climbing the stairs on tiptoe because he could hear Esmé-the-Art-Student chatting to Abi in the kitchen.

It was ridiculous how long it took to send that message, but the answer came quickly: Yep. Cheesy nikes in the bin.

GET THEM OUT! THAT IS THEFT! wrote Max furiously from his bedroom, and now found he had no signal at all, not even when he hung out of his window. He would have to sneak back down again and risk encountering Esmé. He still had not met her. He was dealing with her on the principle of what he had not seen could not exist.

But it was difficult. Day after day, racing up the stairs before he could be spotted from the kitchen. Starving up there till she left. Sometimes Louis could be persuaded to bring him a biscuit. Once Abi had knocked on his door and silently offered tea and toast. But usually he starved; he was terribly hungry now, for instance. Lunch had been a damp and frugal plastic-wrapped sandwich, because the collapse of the bike-repair and car-cleaning business had made him worry about money again. Opposite him, in the dining hall, Danny had gobbled wraps and falafels, bananas and brownies.

Max missed Danny's mum's cooking. He missed Danny too. He was fed up, ravenous, cut off from the outside world; his only decent trainers were in Danny's bin and he hadn't any phone signal. He hovered by his bedroom door, ready to dodge back in if necessary, and a smell like heaven came floating up the stairs. He knew what it was; he had fished it out of the freezer himself that morning. Macaroni cheese toasting in the oven, with tomatoes baking on the top.

Hungry Max forgot his trainers and stood sniffing at the top of the stairs. It smelt cooked. It smelt like it might dry up and burn if it was left a minute longer. He tried to make Esmé leave early by willpower.

It worked.

Max could hardly believe it, but it worked.

The kitchen door opened. There were voices in the hall.

Abi saying, 'Don't fall over Max's bike!' Esmé asking, 'My jacket? Where is my jacket? Ah!'

Max punched the air. He had superpowers. *Hurry up, hurry up, hurry up!* he silently urged Esmé.

He didn't have to wait long.

'*À bientôt!*' he heard her call. '*À bientôt*, Louis!' and then the front door opened and closed and the house was suddenly still.

'Where's everyone?' shouted Max as he headed downstairs, and almost at once heard Louis' voice, droning behind his bedroom door.

'Louis! Come on!' he called.

'Why?'

'Food.'

'I'm singing.'

'Well, shut up and come and eat!'

Louis huffed indignantly down his nose and droned louder, so Max went to look for Abi. She seemed to have done one of her usual vanishing acts. There was no one in the kitchen when he opened the door, but the table was ready for supper, with a fresh loaf of rye bread waiting to be dunked in peppery olive oil, and a bowl of watercress and lettuce to go with the macaroni in the oven. It was a lovely sight. All that was needed, thought Max, now very much happier, was baked beans with the macaroni to make it an entirely perfect meal.

He checked the cupboard for a can, but there weren't any, so he took a handful of biscuits and a chunk of cheese to keep himself going and wandered into the rocking-horse room, where the mobile signal was the best. There he dropped down on the sofa and began firing off a chain of trainer-related threats to Danny. They went with satisfying swiftness, for once. It wasn't until Max sat back to wait for the replies that he noticed how dark the house had become.

Also he had the strangest feeling of being watched. So strange, and so strong, that for at least a minute he sat motionless, his eyes fixed on his phone screen, his nerves flickering with unease.

When he looked up at last, there was a face at the window.

A pale, still face pressed against the glass, eyes half veiled in darkness, breath misting in the cold night.

There, and then gone.

Upstairs, Louis sang on, a thin, eerie drone, but Max, who had frozen in shock, now sprang into panicking action, ran to the front door, fixed the safety chain, shoved across the never-used bolts, top and bottom, and then turned back to the kitchen to do the same there, knocking down his bike on the way.

'Aaaah!' he gasped as a pedal hit his shin, then shoved it aside and hobbled to the back door. There were no bolts on this one, nothing to hold it except the lock, but he grabbed the table (spilling the salad) and managed to wedge it with that.

'Max! Max!' cried Louis in the doorway.

''S'all right,' panted Max, checking the window lock and pulling down the blind. ''S'all right, don't worry! Let me past – Is your bedroom window open?'

He raced upstairs without waiting for an answer, and Louis

ran after him, protesting, 'I tidied! I tidied! Don't mess it all up!'

'There!' said Max, slamming shut the window, closing the curtains against the dark, and scattering all Louis' neat row of star-shaped cat biscuits, lined up like an offering on the windowsill. 'Oh God, what's that?'

There was someone at the door, hammering hard with the heavy iron door knocker.

Max grabbed Louis and held him tight. 'Don't make a sound!' he ordered. 'There's someone weird out there. I saw them at the window.'

Louis stared at him, his eyes beseeching and full of questions.

Thump-thump. Thump-thump, pounded the knocker at the door.

'You stay here,' ordered Max. 'I've got to leave you. I'm going down with my phone.'

Louis' mouth wobbled and wobbled, but he made no sound.

'It'll be OK. The door's bolted and the chain's on . . . I need to find a signal, though. I'm going to ring the police.'

Huge tears began to pour down Louis' cheeks. 'I want Mum!' he wailed, running to the window. 'I want Theo! I want Abi 'n' Esmé! When're they coming?'

At exactly that moment the thumping paused and from down in the street a voice called, 'Louis, where's Max?'

'Abi!' shrieked Louis, then skidded down the stairs, dodged Max's fallen bike and began tugging at the front door handle.

Then Max knew what a fool he'd been.

He had to help Louis with the bolts, and then he had to move the kitchen table so it was a table again, instead of a barricade. Miserably he fumbled to rearrange the lettuce and watercress, found the bread on the floor and picked it up.

'I just thought beans would be nice!' he heard Abi say, sounding completely bewildered, but he couldn't look at her. He couldn't look at anyone, so he concentrated on opening the oven and lifting out the macaroni cheese. He only knew his hands were shaking when a voice behind him asked, 'Maaax?'

Max jumped and spun around, his oven mitt slipped, and bubbling hot macaroni cheese in a blue glazed dish dropped and smashed and splattered at Esmé's feet.

Esmé gasped and Abi shrieked and Louis started crying again.

Max stood transfixed amidst the shrieking and the broken china and macaroni (smelling more wonderful than ever, unattainably wonderful) for what felt like hours. Hours and hours, struck speechless, with Esmé there in front of him.

'Staring,' said Abi afterwards.

'I didn't mean to stare.'

'And not saying a word.'

'I couldn't think.'

'And then you ran away. We only went to the shop to buy beans. We forgot to take a key. Esmé took one tiny look through the rocking-horse-room window and . . .'

'Oh shut up.'

'. . . you barricaded the house and terrified Louis and dropped the macaroni cheese and ran away!'

It was true. Max had bolted, out into the windy street, past the noodle shop and the little grocery. He had run and run, far into the evening.

He had run all the way to Danny's house, to Danny's closed door, and there he had stopped. There, too, Theo had appeared like a miracle on his bike in front of him, and had braked and shouted, 'Max!'

Theo got off his bike and walked quietly beside him until Max could manage to look at him and speak, and after that they went back together, phoning ahead to say they were on the way. When they arrived, they found the kitchen tidy and only the faintest smell of cheese in the air. Theo went out and bought wonderful noodles and made them all use chopsticks, and Esmé could do it best, and Abi nearly as well, and Louis put his face right down in his supper and got noodles in his hair.

It became a sort of party.

Max ate noodles and juggled chopsticks and pretended he was at the party too, but he wasn't. In his head he was still struck speechless, with Esmé in front of him. Esmé, seen at last: swinging dark hair, scooped-neck black T-shirt showing bright pink bra straps, tight black jeans, and silver ballet shoes splattered all over with macaroni cheese.

All night it was the same. Long after Esmé had gone home, sent in a minicab by kind, tired Theo, and Abi was asleep, and Louis was asleep, and Iffen, stretched out beside Louis was asleep, and even the wind was sleeping too, not an ivy leaf moving, Max lay wide awake, staring out into the dark.

All he could think of was pinkness and blackness and silver shoes and the way she had said his name, slow and questioning: 'Maaax?'

He didn't know if it was the best night of his life or the worst; it was impossible to tell.

CHAPTER EIGHT

Since Polly went away no one had told Louis to change his pyjamas, so he hadn't. Very early on Saturday morning he came uninvited to Abi's room and sat on Abi's bed in them. Every breakfast he had eaten since Polly left was recorded on the front, he'd used the sleeves as handkerchiefs, and the night before had stored rescued macaroni cheese in the pockets.

'Go away,' said Abi, outraged.

Louis looked very surprised and asked, 'Why?'

'I don't want visitors, that's why.'

'I thought you might want to see my best thing?'

'No thank you.'

'You don't know what it is yet. Wait, look! I can put both my big toes in my mouth at once.'

'DON'T!' said Abi, but he did it anyway and then asked, rather muffled, 'Isn't that good?'

'It's completely gross,' said Abi.

'Oh,' said Louis, disappointed, and then, after a moment or two, 'Mum said it was brilliant when I did it for her.'

'She only said that because she's your mother.'

'Your mum's dead, isn't she? Poor Abi.'

'Shut up and mind your own business.'

'My dad sodded off,' said Louis with satisfaction.

Despite herself, Abi had to fight down a splutter of laughter.

'That's what Mum said,' continued Louis. 'Sodded off because he couldn't hack it. I'm not supposed to say it, though. Anyway, it's good because now I've got Theo instead. And you're my sister.'

'I am not your sister and don't you dare put your disgusting spitty feet on my quilt.'

'All right,' said Louis, and rubbed them on Abi's bedside rug instead.

'You are truly disgusting,' said Abi severely, 'and you should put those horrible pyjamas in the washing basket.'

'What, now?'

'YES NOW!' said Abi.

Louis slid off the bed and disappeared, but came back much too quickly.

'I've done it,' he said cheerfully.

'Get out!' screeched Abi, and Louis' happy face contorted and she heard him run down the stairs and dive through his bedroom door and begin singing, 'Iffen, iffen, iffen . . .' with a sort of squeaky urgency that filled her with dismay.

Abi rolled over in bed and hid her face under her pillow. Louis. His pyjamas. His wet toes. And, *Your mum's dead, isn't she?* and, *Now I've got Theo.*

Not to mention, *And you're my sister.*

But the obliging way he had hurried to the washing basket.

80

And returned; pink, pleased . . .

Abi, still beneath the pillow, sighed because she had thought when they moved things would become all right, and they hadn't, and lately she couldn't even read to escape any more. Lately, she had become wary of books.

Which was ridiculous.

And unbelievable.

Mad.

Had anyone, ever, drowned in a book?

Or toppled over a cliff in a wobbly bus?

Or in any way damaged themselves from a reading-related accident?

Abi knew who would know.

She found Theo in the rocking-horse room, walking around with his hands behind his neck and his nose in the air.

'You've started doing Polly's yoga,' Abi said, slightly accusingly.

'Wrong, but I might,' said Theo. 'I'm trying to get my head round this ceiling. I'd be in dead trouble if I knocked a bit off.'

'A bit off your head?'

'No, no. Well, yes, that too. Now then, it's only just seven on a Saturday morning. What gets you up and down so early?'

'Books,' said Abi. 'I wanted to ask you something about books.'

'Hmm?' asked Theo, doing some stretches against the panelling (which he was gradually polishing, square by square in every odd moment he had).

'At the hospital,' said Abi, 'do people ever come in because of books?'

'They'd be disappointed if they did,' said Theo. 'We're a bloodbath-and-counselling service, not a library. We've got a few kids' picture books and Willy-the-Mop keeps a stack of papers for the drunks to sit on, but that's about it. Don't roll your eyes!'

'Yes, but do people ever come in because they've had *accidents* with books?'

'Ah,' said Theo, stopping his stretches and lowering himself down against the wall to sit in a proper listening position. 'Right, got you! Yes. Yes they do. Books are dangerous things. Bookcases fall on people all the time. Dopes drop them on their toes and come in hopping. Nutters read them walking down the street and collide with lamp posts. Babies eat them. And there are many, many accounts of people being shut in libraries after closing time. They generally get injured breaking their way out.'

'But,' said Abi, more patiently because she was sitting beside him now, and his shoulder was nice and warm, 'what about accidents from *reading* books. Actually reading them. From the reading. Not lamp posts and things.'

'Less common, but possibly even more dangerous,' said Theo, giving her an enthusiastic hug. 'There's reading by candlelight when you fall asleep and catch fire. Reading while cooking; cookery books cause a lot of knife-related injuries!'

'What?'

'Oh yes! Chopping parsley while you check what you've

got to do next? Whoops! Recipe for disaster! And, of course, there's all the folk that get struck by lightning reading under a tree in a thunderstorm. Not to mention the kids who come with everything from splinters to concussion from trying to get through the backs of wardrobes. And don't get me started on Harry Potter and whiplash. You would *not* believe the number of people running luggage trolleys into brick walls!'

'Yes, but . . .'

'Sitting on broomsticks and launching themselves out of bedroom windows! Bothering dragons!'

'Stop it!' said Abi.

'What?'

'Being silly.'

'Me?' asked Theo, in a very high voice with his eyebrows raised. It was Saturday morning and he had two whole days ahead away from the hospital, which hadn't happened for weeks. He couldn't help being silly.

Abi said, 'I just want to know, if you believe in . . . in . . .' She paused. 'Not magic . . .' She paused again.

'Not magic?'

'No.'

'Go on.'

'If someone was reading a book about a bus, it would be impossible for them to be *on* the bus, wouldn't it?'

'I'm keeping up, Abi, I think.'

'Or if it was about the sea and then, while they were reading, they fell. Or slipped, into the sea.'

'Are we still on the bus?' interrupted Theo.

'No. We're in here. This room. In this house.'

'You still like the house?' asked Theo a little anxiously, and he looked around at the bare old-fashioned room, with the empty fireplace, and the ivy-leaf shapes at the window and he remembered Polly's thoughts of eeriness.

'It's like a house in a book,' said Abi, and reached out a hand to touch the carved panelling. 'You're not listening properly. I was talking about the sea. Reading about the sea and then falling into the sea . . .'

'Reading about the sea and then falling into the sea?' repeated Theo.

'Yes.'

'The actual wet stuff?'

'Not right in,' said Abi, and became quiet, baffled by the impossibility of explaining. Theo, however, looked thoughtful, and then very pleased and exclaimed, 'I know what! We'll go!'

'Go where?'

'Pop across to Southend or somewhere!'

'Do you mean to the real sea?'

'Why not?'

'Just me and you?'

'Abi! Have a heart. Whole family needs a cheer-up if you ask me!'

'Max never will,' said Abi. 'Not after last night. He'll probably never come out of his room again.'

'He ate his noodles.'

'Dying inside.'

84

'We've all been there,' said Theo, not denying it. 'Pancakes first and then we'll see.'

Pancakes brought the boys downstairs, first Louis (dressed, Abi was thankful to see) and then Max, pale from his sleepless night. Theo immediately handed him the frying pan and the jug of batter, set Abi slicing oranges, Louis cupboard-hunting for chocolate spread, raspberry jam and squirty cream, and sat down himself to write a list.

'Jackets,' he said. 'Hats, all that. Twopence pieces for the arcades, spare socks, a towel or two, bucket and spade we can buy there if we want them, what else do you take to the beach, Louis?'

Louis fell out of the cupboard in surprise.

'The beach at the seaside?'

'Lovely day for it,' said Theo calmly. 'Can you find a football, Max, do you think?'

'Are you for real?' asked Max.

'Yep.'

'Why?'

'Got a day off,' said Theo. 'Day off, and the sun's out. Where else?'

'When?'

'Driving over soon as you're ready,' said Theo.

And an hour or so later, they did, heading straight into the east wind and screaming seagulls and there they wore themselves into peace with ridged sand and bare feet in icy, lace-edged waves and later football, with Theo as the goalie and the sea for the goal. As they left, Abi picked up seashells, and when Louis noticed, he picked them up too, jubilant to find three yellow periwinkles and two halves of a cockleshell, still joined in the middle.

'Abi can have the yellow ones,' he said, showing them to Theo. 'No! Abi can have them all. I'll just have ordinary things in my other pocket. There!'

He organized his jacket busily, explaining, 'I've made a first-best pocket for Abi and a second-best one that already has a little hole in for me.'

Later he found a large dead starfish.

'Which pocket is that going in?' teased Theo.

Louis emptied his first-best pocket shells into his hat, put his second-best pocket shells into his newly emptied first-best pocket, and put the starfish in his now vacant second-best pocket. Then he carried the hat proudly to Abi.

'No, no!' she protested, saw his eyes and changed her mind.

'Thank you. They're beautiful. Thank you,' she said.

It was too cold for sandcastles, but the arcade was warm. Theo collected two pounds' worth of twopence pieces and shared them out. Louis was the first to lose his money and Abi was the last. Twice she made a breathless fortune, and twice it was taken from her. Max changed fifty pence of his own, in order to show her how her timing was wrong, but in the end they all agreed that the machines were probably rigged.

'Food,' said Theo, when all was lost, and so they straggled back to the car with parcels of chips, and the wonderful smell of curry sauce floating behind them like a banner. A white highway cat ran out of a pub doorway and waylaid them under an early pink street lamp. They raced for the honour of giving it the first chip, blowing to cool them, charmed to hand over the best and crispiest. The cat reached up for them one by one with endearing white paws.

'I wish it was a stray and we could take it home,' said Abi.

'I think it is home,' said Theo.

Louis shifted his starfish in his pocket and thought of Iffen. Would Iffen like a white cat friend? Was Iffen ever lonely?' *He has me*, thought Louis. *I have Iffen; he has me. So it's fair.*

Theo was right. The white cat was home. When the chips were finished, it wound briefly round their legs, crossed to a birch tree, cleaned its paws by raking the bark with extended needle-sharp claws, glanced over its shoulder as if in farewell and sauntered away. They felt suddenly alone and cold.

'We should be on our way too,' said Theo, and no one disagreed.

On the journey home the boys fell asleep, Max in the front with the road atlas on his knees. Louis in the back, tipping slowly sideways on to Abi until his head rested against her sandy, damp jeans. He was dreaming. Once he reached out a hand, said, 'Mum,' quite clearly, opened his eyes and found Abi instead. 'Sorry-is-it-all-right?' he murmured, and Abi said, 'Yes, it's fine.'

Theo heard and turned his head to smile at her.

Abi looked down at Louis. There was no substance to his curls, they were as light as feathers and his bones were thin. She wondered if Polly missed him, and thought she probably did. *I would miss him*, she thought, surprising herself. She surprised herself too, in longing for her book. The sea air had blown her thoughts back into a much more sensible state. She thought of her sunlit ocean and had a good idea. She would find the end, check and double check that the voyage had finished with no one drowned, and then go back to where she had stopped and begin again.

Theo hummed as he drove, blurrily, like a weary bee. He thought that the seaside had been a good idea, and when he got his second wind he'd make a start on the ceiling. *So far so good*, thought Theo, and he smiled as he glanced at Max nodding beside him. Old Max, taking a break from the shock of Esmé. *Nothing ever the same again*, thought Theo, remembering the first girl who had stepped into his consciousness, stopped his heart and restarted it. Like stepping off a cliff into deep water, what with the plunge and the shock and the half-drowned scrabble to get your head above water again, and then the sun in your eyes . . .

'Nearly home,' he said, an hour later, and his carload of passengers began to shake themselves awake. It was dark, but the Narnia lamp was shining for them, gilding the shadowy ivy and spilling pale gold on to the steps. Hunger besieged them, so they ate scrambled eggs with buttered toast and tomatoes for vitamins. Then they staggered around the kitchen, loading the dishwasher while Theo got out brushes and paint in the rocking-horse room and climbed on to a kitchen chair. He'd vacuumed the ceiling, but even so the plaster leaves and roses were grubby and stained, grey from dirt, brown from spider nests. Theo painted one with thick cream paint, and it looked so good he painted another, and another and another.

'Can I help?' asked Abi.

'Can you reach?'

Abi stood on a chair to test, but she couldn't.

'Never mind,' said Theo, busy amongst his roses.

'Why're you doing it so fast?' asked Louis.

'Want to get it done before your mum gets back.'

'Soon?'

'Soonish.'

'Tomorrow?'

'Tomorrow we are shopping so's to stuff the cupboards with lovely food and then we're cooking Granny Grace's special coconut curry and I'm making ice cream after with deep-fried Mars bars like they eat in Scotland.'

Louis asked him very doubtfully if he knew how.

'Do I know how?' asked Theo, scornfully. 'I was born there! You're yawning, Louis! What about bed? I'll be up to give you a hug when I've done a bit more here.'

'I will if Abi does,' said Louis, and Abi went quite willingly because she wanted to read, and that left Max alone with Theo.

Max had worked out that he could probably reach the ceiling if he tried, but he didn't. He sat on the sofa and searched for Esmé on Facebook and found she didn't exist. He did find a website where you could learn French for free and he studied it for several minutes in increasing despair, and then he watched Theo for a while. He felt the way a person does when there are two people in the room and one is being heroic and the other isn't.

Theo looked down at him from his ceiling and said proudly, 'Looking good, you think?'

Max nodded, and then asked, for the sake of something to say, 'Shouldn't you have got the chimney swept first?'

The results were spectacular. Theo, an open tin of paint in one hand, a paintbrush in the other, stepped backwards off the chair in dismay, flung up his arms to save himself and created a deluge that splattered to the ceiling and covered most of the floor.

'I'm glad I didn't do that,' observed Max, wiping paint blobs from his face.

Theo's expression changed from extreme surprise to sudden laughter. It was so infectious that Max could not help grinning too. The clean-up took them till nearly midnight and by the time the two of them staggered off to bed, the heroic levels were much more balanced between them.

That night, Abi emptied her seashells into an old pencil case, sniffed the sea smell that came with them, and opened her book. Then, skipping the long damp passages scattered between sails and storms, encountering flying fish by day and phosphorescent whales by night, she crossed the South Pacific, was stranded on a coral reef and finally waded ashore to discover windblown palm trees beneath a brilliant blue sky.

Deep in the dark she woke to find sand on her pillow and

a new seashell in her hand, white, speckled with caramel markings, rose pink inside.

'Did you find it yesterday?' asked Louis, when he saw it the next morning.

'Yes,' said Abi, turning the shells, and admitting the magic at last. 'Yes, I found it yesterday, but on a different beach.'

CHAPTER NINE

Towards the end of Sunday, after the shopping (during which Louis wandered off so many times he came perilously close to being strapped into the trolley's toddler seat), and the curry (broccoli instead of cauliflower was a mistake) and the deep-fried Mars bars (disaster) and the great washing of school uniforms (which had been completely forgotten and now would never be dry in time for morning) and a phone call from Polly that sounded like fragments of broken glass colliding on another planet – towards the end of that tempestuous day, Louis glimpsed Mrs Puddock and started screaming.

'Louis?' asked Theo, very gently, down on his heels so he could look into Louis' face. 'This is a bit daft, isn't it?'

Louis pushed Theo hard, so that he toppled over backwards, then ran up to his bedroom.

'Louis?' said Abi, a few minutes later, from outside his closed door.

Louis opened his door just wide enough to look out at her. His face was white, with tear-stain blotches round the eyes.

'I've brought you toast and chocolate spread. Pink milk and a banana.'

Louis opened his door slightly wider.

'And I've downloaded a really funny cartoon about frogs and toads and tadpoles.'

Louis took the toast, the pink milk and the banana, and then he shut the door again.

Iffen visited early that night. Iffen the hungry, the untamed, Iffen the great warmth when the shivers came. Louis opened his window and heard him. The sound of his arrival was like gusts of wind before a storm, and the feeling in Louis' heart when he heard it was the moment before a firework rocket explodes into stars.

Except for the sound in the ivy, his movements were silent. He prowled like an animated shadow. He smelt wonderful, part smoke, part caramel. His leaps looked like slow motion. When he turned his head to look at Louis, an amber power traced patterns on the nerves beneath Louis' skin. From his very first visit he had taken ownership of Louis' room, Louis' bed and Louis' mat (on which he sharpened his claws).

'Iffen,' said Louis. 'What if Mrs Puddock grows?'

Iffen glanced at him with contempt.

Iffen banished loneliness. His arrogant sorting through the offerings on the windowsill made Louis smile. Either they vanished completely, or were flicked scornfully into the ivy. They were not enough. Lately Iffen had taken to bringing his own supplies.

At first Louis had not understood. The night he found a squirrel in the centre of his patchwork mat, still warm, with surprised dead eyes and a bloody nose. He behaved very badly.

'Yuck!' said Louis, and picked it up and flung it out of the window.

Then, right before him, Iffen swelled to twice his size: a monster cat-thing, arched back, flattened ears and a bottle-brush tail. '*Tcha!*' spat Iffen, a furious sound that backed Louis flat against the wall.

'I'm sorry, I'm sorry!' begged Louis, with his arms in the air like a boy held hostage, but Iffen was gone, back out through the window and running down the ivy wall as if it were not vertical. A minute or two later, Louis heard terrible crunching from the shadows beneath.

I suppose he was very, very hungry, Louis had thought remorsefully, and had redoubled his food offerings. This was so difficult, his family being vegetarian, and Iffen being quite the reverse, that he invested a vast amount of his pocket money in a box of dog biscuits, the large ones shaped like bones. These were well received. Iffen disappeared with the first under Louis' bed, from whence came growls and munching.

'Now you needn't catch any more squirrels,' said Louis, and was not pleased when Iffen appeared with one the very next evening, dangling from his jaws like a thin grey moustache.

Iffen had put the squirrel in the middle of Louis' pillow.

Then they had both looked at it.

In Louis' head had come a sudden great longing to pick up the pillow, squirrel included, and hurl it into the night, to evict the murderer after it, to slam the window, draw the curtains and delete all memories of owls, nowls, squirrels, cat-things and pigeons. Louis guessed now who had left the two white feathers in the nest in the ivy, and he knew without doubt that the occupant had not, as he had previously believed, come alive and flown away.

And now this squirrel on his pillow. His own private dinosaur pillow. Louis put his hands on his hips and glared at Iffen and commanded, 'Take it away!'

But Iffen had only rearranged the squirrel a little, like someone rearranging the bow on a parcel, and then Louis realized, all in a moment, that he had been given a gift.

'Oh, Iffen,' he murmured, melting with love, and he had picked up the squirrel and mimed eating it, beginning at the tail, like a long limp grey baguette.

Now Louis had a surprise to offer in return. His starfish from the beach halted Iffen mid-prowl. He sniffed it with caution, ears laid flat, gave Louis a questioning, amber glance, and sniffed it again.

'It's a starfish,' said Louis.

Iffen hooked it up on one claw, held it enquiringly for a moment, then bent his head. His jaws moved twice. That was all.

It had been a large and leathery starfish, bigger than Louis' hand.

'Gosh,' said Louis, a little shakily.

Later that night, lying cramped under the quilt, not quite daring to stretch out his legs, Louis looked at Iffen, outlined against the shadowy window. He wondered how he could ever have believed him to be a nowl.

CHAPTER TEN

Max was in his bedroom, talking to his mirror. It was Monday and he had rushed home from school, showered, cleaned his teeth and dug out his best jeans and T-shirt, the Snoop Dog one that Danny's eldest brother had once remarked was cool. Now he was practising the words he needed for Esmé. He said to the mirror, 'I'm sorry about dropping the pasta on Friday. It was stupid.'

It had taken him two days and two nights to put these sentences together, and he still wasn't sure they were right. Pasta or macaroni? Sorry, so sorry, or really sorry? To grin, as if it was almost funny? To look humble? To remark casually, as if he had only just remembered?

Max tried again, with macaroni and grinning, and then with pasta and humble, and then macaroni and casual, and then with really sorry, pasta and slightly raised eyebrows. Max did this twice and thought it was probably the best. He wished he could have worn his sunglasses, because he felt much more confident with them on, but he couldn't because it was winter and indoors. He tried the words through one more time and then went down and said them.

Esmé had, as usual, walked Louis home, helped him find a snack, switched on the kitchen TV, watched five minutes of cartoons with him, and then opened her enormous art book and become immersed in her work. She looked blankly at Max after he had spoken, so he coughed, rearranged his eyebrows (which seemed to have stuck in the raised position) and attempted to juggle with two oranges from the fruit bowl.

Esmé's look became very puzzled.

'So are we OK now?' asked Max.

'*Pardon?*' asked Esmé.

Max repeated his words again, quite loudly, with macaroni this time and no eyebrow control at all.

'Ah!' said Esmé, nodding to show she now understood (obviously, Max realized, her weekend had not been harrowed by recurring memories of dropped pasta). 'I think next time you please stay and clear up.'

'Definitely, definitely!' agreed Max (in – oh, horrors! – a fake American accent), retrieved the oranges from under the table, held one each side of his head to make cartoon ears and then put them back in the fruit bowl.

'*Pas gentil*,' remarked Esmé, taking them out again.

Max was very pleased to have been spoken to in actual French, although he had no idea what she meant. '*Oui, oui*,' he said, suddenly wonderfully happy. 'Can I see what you're drawing? Louis, does she mind?'

'She does not mind,' said Esmé, rolling her eyes. '*Voilà!*'

It was the first time Max had seen any of Esmé's art. Looking at it made him feel sorry for her. It was so shabby: huge grey dusty sheets of paper, all scribbled in pastel and charcoal, orange and black, ochre and white. However, he tried not to let what he felt show on his face, and said, 'It's brilliant, what is it? Oh, I can see now . . . Horses?'

'Esmé's book is full of horses,' said Louis. 'Horses and bears, *tous les animaux*.'

'Who taught you French?' asked Max severely.

'*Personne*,' murmured Louis. For weeks now Esmé had spoken to him in French when she couldn't be bothered with English, and he had soaked up the new words without noticing. He had learned to shrug too. He shrugged and began colouring the palm and fingers of his left hand bright orange with one of Esmé's chalks.

'Stop it!' ordered Max, feeling very grown-up. 'Don't waste her stuff. She hasn't got that much. Esmé, I've got a set of multicoloured sharpies you can borrow if you like.'

'No thank you,' said Esmé, laughing.

'She doesn't use things like that,' said Louis.

'You be quiet,' said Max.

'Is true,' said Esmé.

'She does cave art,' said Louis. 'Like cavemen did.'

'Louis, just shut up!' said Max, appalled. 'What do you know about art? You don't understand anything!'

'Stone Age,' said Louis. 'I do understand. I help.' He held out his orange hand to Esmé. She inspected it, frowning a little.

'Water,' she said.

'Yes, and soap,' agreed Max bossily. 'Get to the sink and don't touch anything!'

Louis ignored him, dipped one clean finger of his right hand into his water glass and began swirling his orange chalk into paint.

'Not too much,' said Esmé, sliding her paper dangerously close to him as she spoke. 'No drips! Where I say, OK?'

'OK,' agreed Louis, and then Esmé pointed, Louis reached over, and to Max's absolute horror, slapped his bright orange hand flat on Esmé's drawing and pressed hard.

'LOUIS!' yelled Max.

Louis lifted his hand and showed a perfect print, four fingers, palm and thumb.

'That'll never come off!' exploded Max.

'Little more chalk, little more water, then again,' said Esmé composedly. 'Very good, Louis.'

'All that fuss because I dropped the macaroni cheese,' said Max, outraged, 'then he makes a mess like that and you say very good!'

'I didn't fuss,' said Esmé, and at last she stopped hanging over her awful artwork and looked up at him. Her eyes were dark, crinkled at the corners with laughter. She pushed her hair behind her ears, and he saw black crystal studs, very small. Around her neck a leather thong was threaded with a piece of stone, roughly pear-shaped, smooth and nearly white against her olive skin.

Max's eyes followed the line of the thong down to the stone

and stopped. He became very hot. He thought, *I must look somewhere else quick*. He found himself juggling again, very recklessly, throwing the oranges much too high. It made Louis laugh and when Louis laughed, Esmé laughed, which was actually magnificent and caused Max to suddenly remember some French that he never knew he had. '*Ça va? Je t'aime!*' he cried. 'Is that right? *Bien sûr! Voilà, les pommes orange!*'

His juggling ended abruptly with two hard impacts on the table.

'*Non!*' wailed Esmé.

'Oh God oh God I'm sorry,' moaned Max.

'I'll get a towel,' said Louis.

Chapter Eleven

There was nothing magical about weekday mornings at the ivy house. The air was full of tension with the scurry to be ready for school and work. Max, stoking up with cereal, steeling himself for another day of Danny. Theo, drinking coffee, ironing school shirts that hadn't quite dried, unloading the dishwasher, making banana toast, pumping bike tyres, bothering Louis with his reading book. One damp and chilly morning Abi was down in time to hear:

'Just turn over a page, Louis, show me a word, any word, you don't have to say it out loud. Point, and I'll read it.'

Louis, accidentally interested, pointed. Theo paused his ironing to look.

'Elephant!' he announced triumphantly. 'What d'you know! It's a book about elephants! Why don't they put any elephants in the pictures? They should!'

'It's not a book about elephants, that's why.'

'Elephant! Elephant! Elephant!' Theo declared, pointing at words between gulps of coffee and undoing the rock hard knots in the laces of Louis' shoes.

'None of those words say "elephant"!' said Louis, dancing with impatience.

''Scuse me, Louis, but who can read, you or me? They all say elephant except that one there. That one says "sat". Drink your juice.'

Louis looked at Theo's non-elephant word. He could not help himself. He read it.

'It says "cat".'

'Why'd they put one cat in a whole crowd of elephants?' asked Theo, and then Louis got really mad and shouted that there wasn't a single elephant. It was a book about a cat, that cat in the picture, and it didn't say 'elephant' anywhere. Theo had made it up. It said, 'The cat walked out of the gate.'

'Does it now?' said Theo. 'Is that the post?'

It was. Louis raced to collect it, and came back into the kitchen, shining with pleasure.

'For you!' he said, as he presented a new blue envelope to Abi. 'From Granny Grace! She didn't put a flower in this time, but there's a picture of her sniffing lovely roses!'

'You opened my letter!' said Abi, outraged.

'Only to see if there was another flower.'

'Well, it's spoilt now,' said Abi, pushing him aside to flounce across the kitchen and hurl it in the bin. 'Ruined. Messed about. Covered in cold germs, probably. Sometimes, Louis, I hate–'

'Abi!' said Theo warningly.

'Well, I have to guard everything from him. Rocky. My bedroom. Now Granny Grace's letters. It's not fair.'

'It is fair!' said Louis, sounding very surprised.

'How is it?'

'Because I don't have a Granny Grace and I don't have any letters.'

'Doesn't mean you can have mine,' said Abi.

Louis looked at her, completely baffled. 'I will share with you,' he offered at last.

'You haven't got anything I want to share.'

'I'll share my mum when she comes back.'

Shame made Abi more bad-tempered than ever. She turned away, even when Louis asked, 'Can I have it if you don't want it?' and fished her letter back out of the bin.

'No,' said Theo mildly, taking it from him. 'And no more opening other people's letters, Louis. Abi, look at the time! You're going to miss that bus! Have you got your bag packed? What about you, Max?'

'What about me?'

'Don't go off without your helmet, and it won't do you much good hanging from your handlebars either. Louis, get moving! Teeth, shoes, we need to be out the house! I don't know what we'd do without Esmé and I've been forgetting to pay her so there's an envelope behind the clock. Max, can you see that she gets it?'

Max, who had just worked out that when he was nearly twenty-two Esmé would be only twenty five, which was an entirely reasonable age gap, especially as he was taller than her already and would probably be able to drive then, too, was somehow so horrified by this request that he exclaimed, 'No, I can't!'

Theo raised an eyebrow.

'I'll be back too late to even see her,' said Max. 'Football.'

Theo looked at him. The look said, 'Football takes an hour.'

'And then I'm going to Danny's,' snapped Max, cornered into a double lie.

'You and Danny friends again, then?' asked Theo.

'What's it to do with you?' growled Max, in sudden fury. 'I'm fourteen and I'll do as I like. I didn't ask you to marry my mum! You can boss that loser Louis, but you can't boss me!'

'Why am I a loser?' demanded Louis.

'Elephants, elephants, elephants!' mimicked Max. 'Conned you into reading, didn't he?'

'Dad was helping him!' said Abi, flaring up in defence of Theo. 'Everyone has to learn to read!'

'And you can shut up too!' snapped Max. 'He *can* read. He just doesn't want to. And Mum would be helping him if she hadn't had to go to the other side of the planet to pay the rent on this stupid house you wanted so much!'

'Hey!' protested Theo, but it was no good. Max had grabbed his bike and slammed through the front door in a crashing temper, leaving Louis with his mouth turning ominously down at the corners, Abi seething and Theo clutching his head.

'Handled that well, didn't I?' he moaned. 'Louis, get your shoes on! Abi, your bus!'

It was too late. Abi had missed her bus. She knew there

would be another one along in a few minutes, she only had to wait, although it was not a very nice place to do that, what with the piled bags of rubbish all around the bins next to the bus stop, and the way her hastily packed, half-open school bag was filling with rain. She wished she could repack her bag so it would close, but the only place where she could balance it to do that was the low wall round an empty flower planter. That was a depressing sight. There were fragments of broken glass, and takeaway boxes instead of flowers, and someone had not enjoyed their curry and splattered it everywhere. Abi looked at it in disgust and stepped away, and as she did so, of its own accord, her school bag tipped and dropped half her stuff on the ground. Pens scattered and she had to peel ruined pages of file paper one by one off the wet pavement.

Suddenly Abi had had enough – of the planter and the bus stop and the whole miserable morning.

I'm going home, thought Abi.

Almost back, a shiver of doubt nearly stopped her. She had never deliberately missed school before; she knew people who had, but they had not been brought up by Granny Grace.

'Well, she's in Jamaica now,' Abi told herself. 'Bossing someone else,' and she felt in her pocket for the door key.

She'd never been alone in the house before, nor realized how big it was. She felt as exposed as the only book on a bookshelf, as alone as the last match in a matchbox, as watched as if all Granny Grace's little birds had flocked to settle in the ivy.

The only sound was the dishwasher, swishing through the breakfast dishes.

Abi tiptoed around like a burglar. *What if someone sees me through the windows?* she wondered, and thought she might close the curtains, then straight away changed her mind. What if someone wondered at the curtains being closed?

Granny Grace's letter was there on the table. Abi could hardly pick it up. She'd been horrible to Louis. She'd disgraced Granny Grace, who never in her life had missed a day of school. There was a story about that. *'I and my three sisters loved our school. We did not miss a day. Not even when the storm rains took away our small bridge across the river. We put our school books on our heads and we waded across that river and we were not late!'*

'Are you sure,' Theo would ask, winking at Abi, 'about the rain and the bridge and the river?'

'Quite sure,' Granny Grace would say.

'One day . . .' Theo would tell Abi solemnly, 'you will tell your grandchildren about the time Westminster Bridge washed away, and you waded across the Thames and . . .'

Then Granny Grace would flounce out of the room to fetch her photograph box and find the picture of the small bright stream that was proof, she told them, that her memory was true, and Abi would nod consolingly, and say, 'I believe you, Granny,' and Granny Grace would say lovingly, 'My sweet Abigail.'

To read a letter from Granny Grace was almost to hear her voice.

Abigail, my lovely girl, your daddy tells me that you are helping him in every possible way. I am very proud and happy . . .

Abi, feeling guiltier than ever, put the letter down again and looked around for a possible way to help, right then, at that moment. There were breakfast crumbs on the kitchen floor. She thought she might vacuum them up, and then remembered the noise of the vacuum cleaner, and instead swept them up silently with a dustpan and brush. The kitchen bin rattled when she opened the lid to drop them in, and she jumped.

'*Eerie,*' she had overheard Polly say to Theo.

Yes.

It was a little better up in her own room. No one could glance through that high window, and notice she was home. Not if she didn't switch the lights on, anyway. She supposed even her fairy lights would show from outside. She thought she'd better not play music either.

The house creaked its daytime creaks. They sounded like people leaning on walls.

Thankfully, Abi remembered that she had her school bag with her, full of damp paper, cereal bar wrappers, odd PE socks, and hurriedly done homework: Maths and Spanish and English. She got it all out, sorted the litter, paired the socks, and did the homework over again, this time to Granny Grace standards, rewriting the maths and checking the answers, whispering the new Spanish words until they stuck in her head, opening the book they were reading in English: Anne Frank, *The Diary of a Young Girl.*

Abi's class had been working on it all term, reading excerpts, drawing plans of the house and writing their own diary entries. They had even role-played an afternoon in the annexe. Abi had been Margot, Anne's big sister. 'Anne, half the time, you drive us ALL CRAZY!' she had shouted. Her friends had clapped, but then the teacher had made her do it again, quietly, which ruined the moment.

All these things Abi had done in school, in warm, light classrooms, with cheerful groups of friends. What she hadn't done was curl up in a quiet place, and read, starting at the beginning, with Anne's birthday presents, and her cookies shared at school with friends, and progress, slowly at first, but then faster and faster, by way of clumsy sewn-on yellow stars, vanishing classmates and trembling secrets, to the narrow wooden staircase that led to the secret attic rooms where no one must know she was hiding.

Oh, Anne, thought Abi, huddled on her bed, wrapped in her quilt, and now she knew that her English teacher was right. There would have been no raised voices in those cramped, hidden rooms. However angry, scared or hurt, they would have whispered.

The morning passed. Abi tiptoed down to the kitchen for a handful of biscuits, dithered in the bathroom about flushing the loo, and hesitated on the landing, listening to a sound like slow breathing that came from Louis' room. It was, she realized gradually, the wind in the open window, sucking the curtains in and out.

Louis' door had been hard to open, and then swung suddenly with a crash so loud it stopped her heart. Ivy leaves scattered the floor and bed. Remembering Granny Grace's letter about her helpfulness, Abi gathered them up, smoothed the rumpled quilt and closed the window. As she straightened the curtains, she noticed the yew trees round the churchyard. It was midday, but night still watched from their branches. Abi fled, still clutching the ivy leaves.

I'm never doing this again, she thought, back in her own room. Never, not like this. Shut in and shut out. She wished she could ask Anne, 'How did you bear it?'

Hours became days, and days became weeks, and weeks turned to months and years. And yet, how slowly the time passed.

Thank goodness for the chestnut tree outside the attic window, nearly bare now, a few rusty leaves still clinging, but on clear days there was delft-blue sky between the branches. Small birds came to visit the tree, vanished and returned with friends. They showed their lives in quick, bright fragments. They had seasons, like the trees. Huddled, downy bundles through the winter frosts, and then transformed with spring to slim, swift motion, many voiced in the early mornings, until summer leaves came and hid them in green. There were purple evenings too, and white gulls weaving sky patterns. And the clouds blowing. Stars, now and then. Anne watched them all, and hoped and wrote, opinionated often, frightened often too, wistful, merry, very young and very brave: *'Here is a good beginning to an interesting life . . . I'm young and strong and living through a big adventure . . . I feel liberation drawing nearer . . . every day . . .'*

As Abi read those words, Anne's courage unfurled like a banner and flew over the room. Fear vanished. At the same moment voices called in the hall below, high and clear, 'Abi! Abi!'

Abi dropped her book, and raced down the stairs, being noisy, jumping at the turns. It was Louis and Esmé, shedding jackets, kicking off shoes, smelling of outdoors and school and well-lived days.

'We knew you were here!' said Louis, 'We saw your coat! Are you still mad because I opened Granny Grace's letter? Look at Esmé! She says she's *indisposée.*'

'Esmé?'

'It is nothing,' said Esmé, kissing the air politely by Abi's ear.

'She's not very well,' said Louis. 'She went to a party last night, and now she feels awful. She felt awful all the way home.'

'We'll look after her,' said Abi at once. 'Come on, Esmé, you can have my room and . . .'

'She feels so poorly she nearly left me at After-school Club,' interrupted Louis. 'But then she came because she needs her money.'

Esmé rolled her eyes and gave a beautiful shrug, but somehow she looked frailer than usual, and she said, 'Yes, thank you. I am needing my money today, *s'il vous plaît.* If possible.'

'It is possible,' said Louis. 'Theo left it in the kitchen. I saw him. Wait!'

He disappeared, and came back with it a moment later. '*Pour vous!*' he said graciously, and Esmé smiled and took it, wavered for a moment and said, 'I think I should go now. I think I have to, really.'

'Oh, Esmé!'

'Yes, can you manage, take care, cope? I think so,' said Esmé, and then rushed out of the door without waiting for an answer.

'Goodness!' said Abi as Esmé half ran down the street.

'She had a lot of rum by accident,' said Louis, looking after her.

'Is that what she said?'

'Yes, 'n' now she just wants to lie down and not move. That's why she said can we cope.'

'Poor, poor Esmé.'

'*Can* we cope, Abi?'

'Of course we can!' said Abi, who had found courage that afternoon, brought it back with her, admired it and installed it in her heart.

'Till Max or Theo come back?' asked Louis, and his voice was rather doubtful. 'It'll be dark.'

'It was dark when we first saw the house,' Abi reminded him. 'Don't you remember? And the Narnia lamp switched on?'

Louis' face became suddenly illuminated with memory.

'You loved it,' said Abi, and Louis nodded and said, 'Anyway, Iffen . . .' and raced up to his room.

CHAPTER TWELVE

The first thing Louis saw when he opened his bedroom door was Iffen, impossibly balanced on the windowsill outside. Iffen's amber eyes glared into his so compellingly that, for a moment, Louis hesitated.

The eyes narrowed, the ears went flat, Iffen lifted an imperious beanbag paw and Louis flew to let him in. He drew a deep breath as the aloof, regal head, the bronze-dappled coat, the heavy, black-tipped tail, flowed into the room and settled down on the creaking bed. Each time Iffen seemed more beautiful.

Then, most magically of all, Iffen purred.

It was a sound so deep as to be more felt than heard, a rumbling vibration, an immense echo of comfort, half lullaby, half drum roll. It brought Louis to his knees on the rug beside the bed.

'Oh,' he murmured, as he gazed in adoration, 'you are better'n nowls, better'n a million nowls.'

After a while he became conscious of a rhythm, a regular thud-thud, a heartbeat even deeper than the purring. Louis sat back on his heels and looked into Iffen's face, and then gradually, gradually, it came to Louis that Iffen had become huge.

Iffen yawned. A pink and crimson yawn, which could have fitted Louis' head inside it. Black lips curled to show pale curving fangs. Madly, Louis reached out a finger to touch a pointed tip.

That was a mistake.

Iffen snarled, arched his back and bowled Louis over as he leaped down to the floor. There he stretched out two irritated sets of hooked black claws, and with a lovely canvas-tearing sound, he sliced eight long protesting rips into the patchwork bedside mat.

Louis gasped in shock, which seemed to please Iffen. He flopped down on his side, blocking off the door. Coloured shreds of carpet wool showed between the black pads of his feet. Very delicately, Iffen began removing them with his teeth.

'Louis!' called Abi, from a different world.

'I've got to go,' said Louis.

Iffen blinked.

''Scuse me, please,' said Louis worriedly. 'Else she might try and come in here.'

Iffen lay immobile.

'Louis!' called Abi, a second time.

Louis thought perhaps he could slide the rug with Iffen on it out of his way. He said apologetically, 'Sorry,' and picked up a corner and pulled.

118

Nothing happened.

Louis heaved again, two-handed, watching Iffen warily. The amber gleam beneath the half-closed eyes looked amused. The black lips smiled, with a glimpse of fang at each corner. The rug moved at last, just enough so that Louis could edge round it.

At the door he paused, and looked down. He had never known before that love could be a weight. He felt bowed with it, the great warmth and the power and the joy. He felt terrified too. He didn't know how it had happened, he hadn't seen it coming, but he knew, beyond doubt, that Iffen had grown too big.

Abi had found a crisp brown leaf in her room, light as paper, chestnut-coloured. It was just a dry fragment, but it might have blown from a winter tree in Amsterdam. She had folded it between the pages of her book and gone down and made toast for herself and Louis, spread it with raspberry jam and called him from the bottom of the stairs. When he arrived, he seemed bothered, and he stood very close to her, looking into her face with his silvery eyes.

'What's wrong?' she asked. 'Is it Granny Grace's letter? I'm sorry I got so mad.'

He shook his head.

She pushed the plate of toast towards him, but he didn't seem to notice. He said, 'Abi?'

'Yes?'

'You know when I wanted a nowl?'

'I remember.'

'Iffen came.'

'Iffen?'

'He came through the ivy to my window.'

'An owl?' asked Abi, incredulously.

'No'.

'What then?' asked Abi.

'A cat-thing. Perhaps magic,' whispered Louis.

Abi looked at him, remembering salt and seashells, the lurching bus, the chestnut leaf and the lonely fear of the afternoon. Remembering Granny Grace's green magic.

'Do you believe me?' asked Louis, and she nodded.

'He's got very big,' continued Louis, all in a rush. 'I couldn't step over him. He's up there now, in my room.'

'Will you show me?' asked Abi, and saw the relief on his face.

Halfway up the stairs he asked, 'Are you brave, Abi?' and Abi, who had brought more than a dry brown leaf back from her time in the Amsterdam attic, said, 'I'm braver than I was!'

'Good,' said Louis.

Outside his bedroom, with his hand on the door handle, he paused again to say, 'We mustn't put the light on. He doesn't like it when I do. I'd better go in first . . . Oh!'

While he was speaking, he had gently opened the door and now his voice was soft with relief. 'It's all right!' he murmured. 'Look!'

At first Abi could see nothing, just the room as she had left it after she'd closed the window earlier, nothing changed at all except the slightly rumpled bed.

Although perhaps a little more than slightly rumpled, she realized, peering into the gloom.

Perhaps, you might say, heaped.

Louis' bed appeared to be occupied by a great, billowy shadow. A dim softness of translucent golden grey. Almost as if a smoky evening cloud had drifted in through the window and settled there to rest. Abi looked, and looked again, and then jumped back in alarm and gasped, 'Louis!'

The cloud was breathing, and it wasn't a cloud. It was a very big, heart-stoppingly big cat-thing.

At the zoo there was a terrace on which lions dozed in the sun, right beside a window where visitors could gaze. Abi had paused there once, one step and one thickness of glass away from the rounded bellies, the huge relaxed pads, the slow breathing nostrils.

Now the glass was gone.

It wasn't a tiger – it wasn't striped – nor a lion, not with that blotched coat; not a lynx, much too large for a lynx. A leopard? A cheetah? What was it, what was it?

If it wasn't a dream.

From its tail tip to its extended front paws it was the length of Louis' bed. It stretched, blinked, raised its head, glanced at Louis, saw Abi.

Its gaze stayed on Abi, unwelcoming.

'Iffen,' said Louis, once again kneeling on his bedside rug, his small face perilously close to those paws, 'Iffen, I brought Abi.'

In a dream, it's hard to move. It's hard to think. It's hard to speak. Abi shook off the dream-feeling and gathered her wits.

'Louis, get back!' she whispered. 'Come back, right back, slowly to me. The door's still open. Duck under my arm. I'll come out straight after. We can telephone the zoo . . .'

'The zoo?' asked Louis, laughing at the ridiculousness of such an idea.

'Or the police . . .'

'But I love him,' said Louis, as if that changed everything.

Perhaps it did, thought Abi, and stepped a little closer.

'He used to be quite small . . .'

Iffen's length covered the bed; he smelt of smoke, caramel, charcoal, crushed green ivy and winter air; and yet Abi asked, 'Is he *real*, Louis? What would happen if I touched him?'

'I don't know,' said Louis. 'Don't.'

'All right.'

In the summer, fox-cub watching, Abi had learned something useful. It was that animals do not like a direct gaze. She remembered that lesson now, and carefully looked away from Iffen, absorbing him in glimpses, assembling a patchwork picture in her mind.

There was something familiar about him. Something she'd seen before. This cat. This great cat. This grey and gold and charcoal-shaded cat . . .

All at once, Iffen rose and turned and was gone, out of the window and leaping through the ivy.

'That's what he does,' said Louis, and sighed.

The smell of crushed ivy was still all about them, and Abi couldn't yet grasp what she'd seen, except somehow, once again, there had been magic in the house.

'Does he come every night?' she asked.

'Not every.'

'And no one else has seen him?'

Louis shook his head. 'Only you. He jumped right past Max once, when he came in, but Max didn't notice him. And one night I woke up and Theo was just closing the door, and Iffen was right beside me on top of my quilt. But Theo didn't see him either.'

That was something Abi could almost understand. 'When I was little, I had an invisible dog,' she told Louis. 'No one could ever see him. But I could. I always knew where he was and I used to make space for him to sleep on my bed. I called him Roly. I used to paint pictures of him. He had brown ears and a brown patch on his back and his tail was pointy and he had fat knees.'

Abi paused. Why had she painted him like that? Because she saw him that way? Or had she seen him like that because she'd painted him that way?

'Couldn't even Granny Grace see him?'

'No. But once she fell over him. She was just about to step on him when I shouted out to warn her and she tripped and fell right over him.'

'Did she see him then?'

'No.'

'Why not?'

Abi knew the answer to that. She had worked it out years before. 'Because she didn't believe he was possible.'

'Was he sort of magic?'

'Yes, I suppose he was,' admitted Abi. 'Perhaps you could have seen him.'

'Like you can see Iffen?'

Abi nodded.

'What happened to Roly?'

'I don't know. He stopped coming. I couldn't always make him come when I wanted. Can you always make Iffen come?'

Louis shook his head.

'Louis, I couldn't touch Roly. I wanted to, but I never could. Can you touch Iffen? Is he real enough to touch?'

Louis paused, thinking. Was he? He was real enough to whack the window till it shook. To sag the bed until it creaked. To slice a rug, to block a door. But had he, Louis, actually ever touched him?

'He yawned,' he told Abi at last, 'and I tried to touch his tooth.'

'His *tooth*?'

'It looked so long and shiny. But I couldn't.'

'Good,' said Abi thankfully.

'Why?'

'It would be scary if you could touch him,' said Abi, 'but, if you can't, he's just an . . . an –' she stretched back her mind to remember what Granny Grace used to call Roly – 'an illusion!'

Abi sounded so relieved that some worried part of Louis also relaxed. He didn't know what an illusion was, but he had great faith in Abi.

Already the shock of Iffen was leaving her. He was gone and, just as when the books were closed, the memory was fading, like a very vivid dream fades.

'Tell me next time you see him?' she asked, and Louis nodded, but a day passed, and then another, and it was almost a week before Louis arrived in the kitchen late one evening after he was supposed to be in bed. Abi was alone, finishing her homework, and at first she couldn't think what he was talking about when he appeared before her and said crossly, 'I wish I hadn't let you look at him now! What if he never comes back?'

'What if who never comes back?'

'Iffen, of course!'

'Oh! I'd almost forgotten him.'

'*Forgotten him?*'

'I've had loads of homework, and I've been helping Dad . . .'

'You don't love him,' said Louis, and applied his pyjama sleeve to his nose.

'For goodness' *sake*!' complained Abi, so Louis went into the rocking-horse room where Theo was busy. The latest thing to happen there was that Theo had found a friend at work who claimed to like sweeping chimneys and would sort theirs when Theo said the word.

'The sooner the better,' said Theo, thinking of Polly's latest phone call, which had included, amongst the many messages and instructions, the cheerful words 'beginning to wind up'.

'How long?' he had asked, and Polly had said not long, not long, but not a word to Louis because it would only set him off.

'Not a word to any of them,' Theo had promised, and gone into work very jauntily.

'About time she came back,' said his friend when he heard the news, and, in preparation, he lent Theo his huge supply of ancient discarded hospital sheets. Now Theo was hanging them from the light fittings to protect his precious ceiling from soot, and covering the sofa, and draping the walls, right down to the floor. The rocking-horse room was losing its shape and becoming a white shadowed cave.

'I don't like it,' said Louis, hovering barefoot in the doorway.

'Won't be forever,' said Theo cheerfully.

'It's cold.'

'Better take yourself off to your nice warm bed, then,' said Theo, but Louis took himself off to Max's room instead. The door was not properly closed. Louis slid in and saw that Max had his back to him, and his laptop open. Music was playing and Max was singing 'Esmé, Esmé, Esmé, Esmé' in his own invented French accent while drawing neon pink hearts on his laptop screen.

Sniff, went Louis in a moment when Max (and the Kaiser Chiefs) paused to draw breath, and was yelled at for spying

126

and chased away and down the stairs and into his own room, where he comforted himself by sniffing as much as he liked. Also he opened his window and called out recklessly into the dark, 'Iffen! You can come and get Max if you like!' and was almost instantly overtaken by a great surge of greenness and wildness and magic and muscle that bounded up the ivy and over the sill and stood glaring over him like a wild cat genie let out of a much-too-small bottle.

'*Tcha!*' said Iffen, a harsh, angry, questioning sound from the back of his throat.

'I was joking,' said Louis.

Iffen gave him a very unamused look, turned his back and settled down, taking up three-quarters of Louis' bed. Louis, having nothing better to do, got into the remaining quarter, pushed his legs down too far and accidentally shoved Iffen hard.

Wallop! went Iffen's paw down on Louis' shin, and then Iffen jumped out of the window and Louis put his head right under his quilt and did a great deal more sniffing until at last he fell asleep.

CHAPTER THIRTEEN

Everyone had helped with the practical magic of trans-forming the rocking-horse room. Theo had painted the ceiling. Abi had caught and relocated every spider, a very long job. The cleaning and polishing of the wood-panelled walls had been shared between all of them, with Louis responsible for the lowest panels. He had taken this very seriously, becoming absolutely filthy as he worked his way around on hands and knees. Recently, since Theo had hung the walls with dust sheets, his task had become much harder.

'I have to squeeze behind them,' he complained.

'Wait until the chimney's swept and we'll all give you a hand,' Theo told him.

'You said I could do it all by myself,' Louis replied ungratefully.

'Not if it's going to take forever,' said Max.

'You ALL said . . .' protested Louis.

'You get so dirty it's not worth it,' said Abi. 'The time it takes to wash you is longer than the time it would take to polish.'

129

Louis took such a huge, deep, ominous breath at this that Abi stepped backwards and Max said, 'Crikey, let him do it!' while Theo squatted down, took Louis by the shoulders and said, 'Louis, you can do it. All by yourself.'

'I'm going to,' said Louis, and that evening after supper he collected his polish and dusters and crawled behind a dangling sheet.

He soon backed out again. It was the day after he'd summoned Iffen to get Max, and there was still too much magic about. It wasn't nice to be alone in a shrouded room, stuck between a sheet and a dark wooden wall, with the evening black outside the windows. Abi found him hovering in the doorway, clutching a bunch of ivy leaves. He brightened at the sight of her.

'Will you stay in here with me and not go away without saying?' he asked.

'Why?'

'So's I can polish. Just till Theo comes home.'

'Oh, all right,' agreed Abi, and curled up on the sofa with a book from her bedroom, one that she'd been plodding through for days. Louis became busy out of sight: a little ghost-shaped bulge behind the sheets. Every few minutes he called, 'Are you still there, Abi?' and waited till he heard her say, 'Mmmm.'

Max was also occupied. Abi could hear him in the kitchen, torturing Esmé with his home-made French. *I should go and rescue her,* she thought as she turned a page, but after a while she forgot. The sounds faded. She couldn't hear Max any more. Louis was quiet now too; there was just the rustle of the wind in the ivy outside.

It was a wild wind, and grew wilder. It was fierce and dark and snow-laden, impossible to stand against. It numbed Abi's hands and feet and face, outlined her bones in aching ice, and filled her mind with an astonished joy that there should be a world with such a wind unleashed, and that she should be there to feel it.

It froze her to a standstill.

It was Louis who brought her back from that place, screeching her name and pulling her arms. He had wiggled out from behind his sheet when she stopped answering 'Mmmm' to his questions. He found her bent double, and icy.

'She's dead and she won't talk to me,' he'd wailed, running to Esmé and Max in panic, but Abi wasn't dead, only lost in deep cold. They'd taken her into the warm kitchen, wrapped her in the quilt that Esmé had run up to fetch from her bed and hurried to make her hot tea.

At first she shook too much to drink.

'I think you have fever,' said Esmé.

'F-fever!' chattered Abi, her lips and nails still blue.

'What happened, then?' demanded Max.

'It was the book I was reading. It was like I was there.'

'She had snow on her hair!' said Louis. 'I touched it and it melted!'

'Don't be weird!' Max told him impatiently, and Louis said he wasn't weird – Max was weird. Max was weirder than weird, and Max said, 'Snow! Making things up!'

'*Tu es sot!*' snapped Louis, which made Esmé splutter with laughter, and Max became bright red, and there might have been an argument if Theo hadn't arrived just at that moment.

'What's going on here?' asked Theo.

'I thought Abi was dead, but she's come alive,' said Louis, 'and tell Max to stop saying I'm weird!'

Theo rolled his eyes, took Abi's temperature, checked her pulse, listened to four different explanations, demanded to see the book and sent Max and Louis to find it.

'Now tell me what happened again,' he said, when both arguing boys were out of the way. 'I'm guessing you fell asleep?'

'I didn't. I was awake. I was reading in the rocking-horse room and then I wasn't there any more.' Abi paused, trying to remember. 'I was lost and I needed to find my way to somewhere very important.'

'What sort of somewhere?'

'I don't know. I got colder and colder and it was harder and harder to move. Then I heard Louis call.'

Louis had called, and she had turned towards his voice and found his small hot hands clutching hers, and then they had tugged her back home. The storm had vanished and already the memory was fading.

'Found the book!' said Max, reappearing at that moment with Louis in tow. '*The Worst Journey in the World*, it's called. It looks dead boring.'

'Let me see,' said Theo, but it was just an ordinary book, with lots of black-and-white photos of penguins. No snow fell from the pages when they turned them, much to Louis' disappointment.

'I don't know what to think,' said Theo worriedly, looking across Abi. 'I don't know what Pol would say!'

'I'm all right now,' said Abi, untangling herself from the quilt. 'Why do you have to tell her? She would only get worried about nothing.'

Perhaps it had been nothing. It was easy to agree when Max said, 'That room is always freezing. If anyone fell asleep in there, they might easily get frostbite nightmares.'

It was true, they might.

'Sooner we get that chimney swept and a fire in there, the better,' said Theo, cheering up a little. 'And the whole house feels odd tonight, between polish and damp and I don't know what! I noticed it as soon as I opened the front door. Speaking of the door, Max, you and I need to be a bit more careful bringing our bikes in. It's getting pretty badly scratched.'

'Is it?' asked Max, and went to look. Abi followed after him, for no particular reason except to be back in the normal world again, and Louis tagged along because he always tagged along, and there, by the light of the Narnia lamp, they saw the scratches on the door.

They were long, deep grooves.

Max said at once, 'That wasn't me!'

Louis said nothing.

Abi's thoughts swirled and gathered and scattered away again like autumn leaves in a gusty wind. The white seaside cat raking its paws against the tree. Long-ago Roly. Iffen.

Louis. Abi looked at Louis and he looked back at her, blank-eyed and innocent.

'No way I did that,' said Max, very crossly and Theo said from behind, 'No, probably it was me. Just thought I'd mention it. Esmé, it's a dark night out there – I'm going to get you a cab. Is Mrs P. still hanging about?'

Louis swung round to look at him.

'I met her earlier on the path,' explained Theo. 'Just be careful when you go out. Can we shut the door now before the house gets any colder? How are you feeling, Abi?'

'Fine,' said Abi.

'That's good. Max, if you can just see Esmé off, I'll make a call and see how soon we can get that chimney sorted. Louis, bath and bed?'

Louis glanced at the darkness at the top of the stairs.

'I'll go up with you,' offered Abi.

'Great,' said Theo. 'Esmé, I'll say goodnight, then, and thank you very much.'

'Yes, thank you, Esmé,' said Abi, raising a goodbye hand.

Louis suddenly rushed upstairs, rushed down again, flung himself on Esmé and hugged her. Esmé detached herself with the remote look of someone whose thoughts were already halfway home.

'*Au revoir* and mercy!' said Max, on the doorstep, because if Louis could speak French whenever he felt like it, he didn't see why he shouldn't too. '*Et bonne chance pour le weekend.* What's so funny about that?'

'*Rien de tout,*' said Esmé, vanishing so smoothly into the

dark that when Theo asked afterwards if she'd got the cab all right Max had to think before he could answer, '*Oui*.'

'Don't know what we'll do without her,' said Theo absent-mindedly.

Max didn't want to talk about doing without Esmé, so he went off and sprayed his bike chain with special bike-chain lubricant, and there was something about the smell that took him straight back to summer and the bike-repair and car-cleaning business. He missed Danny terribly, Esmé was leaving, his own dad was long gone, five years and more. Suddenly Max had to lean his head against the wall for quite a while, just thinking.

He didn't know how long he stood there, but when he went back into the kitchen Theo was making a giant omelette, stuffing it with grilled cheese and sliced tomatoes, and rolling it into a long baguette.

'I know you had supper, but keep me company,' he said, cutting it into halves, arranging each carefully on a plate, adding crisps and pickled gherkins, and handing one to Max.

It seemed to Max impossible that a sandwich could help when your best friend was your enemy and the only girl in the world was going back to France, but it made him feel much better, anyway.

Upstairs, Abi became efficient, ran Louis a bubble bath, hunted out clean pyjamas, and caught her foot in his bedside mat. That was when she discovered the two sets of long slashes there, straight and clean as if sliced by two handfuls of very sharp knives. Abi picked up the mat, and looked more closely. Under it, carved on the wooden floor, were eight long lines.

Iffen.

Iffen, who until she had seen the scratches on the door that evening, had retreated into shadow land.

It didn't make sense. Never, in all the time she had known Roly, had he left the slightest mark of his presence. No brown-and-white hairs had ever appeared where he slept. No paw print had ever shown where he walked. He had been real enough to trip up Granny Grace and to have his picture painted, but not real enough for that.

For a long time Abi was very still. Then she collected an armload of pillows and quilts and went to the bathroom door. 'Louis,' she called. 'I'm making you a camp in my room tonight. I've got that chair that unfolds into a mattress. Is that OK?'

Absolute silence greeted this, but when she looked round the bathroom door she saw that his eyes were wide open and there were tears rolling down his cheeks. (Never, not even on the darkest nights when she had woken to feel Roly's weight against her legs, never, for one moment, had Roly been frightening.)

'OK?' Abi asked again, and Louis nodded and kept on nodding until she went away.

CHAPTER FOURTEEN

Almost as soon as they had moved in to the ivy house, Polly had offered to help Abi decorate her bedroom. Abi, alarmed, had asked, 'Can I choose the colours?' even before she remembered to say thank you.

'Of course,' Polly had replied, squashing out of her mind the memory of her own twelve-year-old bedroom, where she had insisted on chocolate brown and nothing else, to look like a hobbit hole. 'Anything you like.'

Abi had chosen a silvery grey colour for the stained, flaking ceiling and a faded greenish blue for the walls. At the corners she outlined with chalk a series of small upright trees, bare-branched, and slender. When the outlines looked right she'd filled them in, with the same silver grey as the ceiling, and then she had looped their two-dimensional branches with fairy lights; amber, rose and yellow. In a charity shop she and Theo found some rusty orange denim curtains, and a matching furry mat. These strange colours fitted together so well that Polly sounded and felt remorseful when she said, 'And I painted Louis' old room for you pink!'

'It was all right. Just a bit . . . a bit . . .'

'It was bubblegum pink!' said Polly. 'Sorry, Abi! I love your greeny-blues and golds.'

'One day I'll do the furniture too,' said Abi, 'and then it will be perfect.'

With the lights switched on, and the curtains closed, the room already looked perfect to Louis. His bed was so close to Abi's he could reach out and touch her hand.

'Come and see!' he called to Max when Abi was getting ready in the bathroom, and Max put his head round the door and asked, 'Why are you even here?'

'In case I get frightened of anything,' said Louis, very pleased with himself now he didn't have to face the night alone.

'She's got you for life, then,' said Max. He had hated sharing a room with Louis, but now suddenly he felt so left out it hurt. It made him bad-tempered. 'You're always frightened of something,' he continued. 'Spiders. Beetles. Haircuts. Toads . . .'

'I'm not!'

'Messy bedroom floors. Mum never coming back . . .'

'She is! She is!' screeched Louis, sitting up and flinging first his pillow, and then Abi's pillow, hard as he could at Max, 'Go away!'

'Crikey, calm down!' said Max. 'I never said she wasn't!' and he tossed back the pillows and retreated to his own room with its spare bike wheels and footballs and orange lava lamp. He'd recently added a poster of the Eiffel Tower and thought it all looked very French.

'Shout if you need me,' he'd told Abi when she came up to bed, but Louis and Abi didn't shout; they whispered.

'Tell me more about Iffen,' said Abi. 'When did you see him first?'

'When Mum was here. I thought he was a nowl. He was much smaller then. But he wasn't a nowl, he was a cat-thing. Then Mum went away and Max was always cross and you read books all the time and I kept seeing Mrs Puddock, and Iffen got bigger and bigger . . . Abi?'

'What?'

'What if Mrs Puddock grows bigger and bigger too?'

'Of course she won't. She's just ordinary. Like . . . like . . . that white cat at the beach was ordinary. And the foxes in the summer. Like nearly everything is ordinary.'

'Not the ivy,' said Louis, and from outside they heard the ivy leaves rustle a little, as if in agreement.

Louis spoke again.

'Iffen isn't ordinary. But he's real too. He does real things.'

'Yes,' agreed Abi, thinking of the marks on the door and the slashed patchwork rug in the room beneath.

'Unordinary things are happening all the time now,' said Louis.

'I know.'

'Do you like it?'

'Like it?'

'This time. This unordinary time. I don't know what it's called,' said Louis helplessly. Abi did. Granny Grace had named it long before: '*What a time of green magic!*'

139

Louis' eyes were on hers, waiting for an answer to his question.

Did she like it? Abi's thoughts revisited these last few green magic weeks. She had been stunned, shocked, chilled to her bones. Astonished. Awed. Lost and found. But her dad had a word that he used about his work now and then: 'privileged'. She had also been privileged.

'Yes,' she said at last. 'I do. But sometimes it's scary.'

'Like Iffen,' said Louis.

'Is Iffen scary?' asked Abi, so gently that Louis could whisper, 'Yes.'

After that he was quiet for such a long time that Abi thought he'd fallen asleep until he suddenly reached up a hand and said sleepily, 'I did see the snow on your hair.'

'I did see Iffen,' said Abi, and she stretched down a hand to touch his, and added, 'Night, Louis,' and watched as he fell asleep.

Then for a long time Abi lay awake, listening. Theo creaked up the stairs, peered round the door, blew a silent kiss and creaked back down again. In the next room Max dropped his headphones, releasing a trickle of French conversation, and flopped down on his pillow. There was the sound of wind in the ivy outside, traffic further away, somewhere a dog barking. Did dogs see Iffen?

Where had Louis found Iffen?

The tired house slept, all except Abi. Abi's mind was turning and turning as she remembered.

The strange music in the blizzard wind. The waiting-to-pounce tension of the attic rooms where Anne Frank wrote her diary. The lurch of the balanced bus. The blue horizon of the South Pacific.

The wild, wide encounters of the worlds she'd discovered in books.

And she'd found a chestnut leaf and a speckled shell. The memory of snow in her hair.

And Louis had found Iffen.

'I think,' said Abi to herself, slowly explaining as she began to understand, 'I think, in the beginning, Iffen must have come out of a book.'

Chapter Fifteen

Saturday morning began with Mrs Puddock. Louis, stationed on the doorstep to watch out for Theo's chimney-sweeping friend, caught sight of her unexpectedly and let out such an awful shriek that his whole family came running.

'She's horrible, she eats beetles, I know she does,' said Louis in a loud fearful voice, and Mrs Puddock heard and froze into stillness, her mouth a tremulous smile, her little hands splayed over something that wriggled.

'It's about time you stopped this stupid Mrs Puddock fuss,' said Max, turning back in disgust when he saw what all the noise was about.

'Yes it is,' agreed Abi, remembering Louis' list of fears from the night before.

Mum went away and Max was always cross and you read books all the time and I kept seeing Mrs Puddock, and Iffen got bigger and bigger . . .

Here was one problem she could deal with, at least.

'Wait!' she ordered, dashed back inside and returned holding the shoebox that had once been used to pack air.

'Good girl,' said Theo approvingly as she began to line it with ivy leaves.

Louis and Mrs Puddock watched from opposite sides of the path, their expressions wary and full of suspicion.

'What are you going to do?' asked Louis.

'Take her somewhere safe,' said Abi. 'Hold this box for me!'

'NO.'

'Hold it!' said Abi, and swiped his bum with the lid in such a no-more-nonsense Granny Grace fashion that Louis screwed his eyes tight shut, but did as he was told.

'Careful,' warned Theo anxiously, and Abi was very careful as, with cupped gentle hands she picked up the small creature that was Mrs Puddock and lifted her into the box.

'Look!' she said to Louis.

Louis unscrewed his eyes a little. Then more. Then wide and astonished.

'Put the lid on and don't joggle her.'

He nodded speechlessly.

'I'll be here,' Theo told Abi. 'Shout if you need me.'

'OK. Come on, Louis.' Abi took the box from him and led the way to the yew tree passage. Two minutes later they emerged into the wilderness of the old churchyard, with its fallen trees and dampness, and MARIAN HEPPLE, 1802, AGED 9. A LOVING HEART FOR ALL GOD'S CREATURES.

'She'll be all right here,' said Abi. 'There's ivy, and grass, and she won't get trodden on, and it's away from the road. It's much better than under our hedge. She'll need to hibernate soon, anyway.'

'Need to what?'

'Go to sleep all winter, like they do.'

'Who do?'

'Toads,' said Abi, taking the lid off the box and tipping it gently on to the ground. 'She's only a little toad, Louis. She was never anything else. Polly just gave her a name for a joke. You know that.'

Louis nodded. He did now. Had he always? No, he hadn't.

Mrs Puddock glanced up at them with her gold-spark eyes, took a hesitant step, then another.

'Wait!' begged Louis all at once. 'I want to see! Abi, make her wait! I've haven't looked at her properly yet.'

For a second, maybe two, Mrs Puddock did seem to pause, then, with a rustle of movement, a dry leaf pushed aside, she folded so perfectly into a miniature landscape of stone and tussock that she became invisible as they watched.

'Gone,' said Abi, and Louis cried, 'What'll we do now, Abi?' suddenly forlorn.

They arrived back home to find that the chimney sweeping had already begun. The air was filled with the smell of soot: sour, tar-tasting and dusty.

'Out!' ordered Theo, but the black velvet softness pouring like water into the fireplace was too fascinating to leave. They all three hovered, longing to help, while Theo and his friend shovelled darkness into bin bags. The first bag split with the weight and then soot billowed unconfined, and made them cough and rub their eyes. Louis' nose ran worse than ever, and this cheered him up tremendously because, to his entranced delight, it ran black. One after another they were ordered into the shower, while the bags of soot were loaded into Theo's friend's very dirty van. It was his first visit to the house and the ivy astonished him. 'Magic, or what?' he exclaimed. 'No wonder you got it cheap! You've not been trying to take it down, have you?'

'Nope!' said Theo. 'For one thing, it's not my ivy. For another, life's too short. And, anyway, it's probably holding up the walls! Why d'you ask?'

'Noticed it was dropping a bit, that's all.'

'Wind,' said Theo wisely.

'Ah!' said his friend, but Abi went out to look. It was true that there was a lot of scattered ivy, especially under Louis' window. Iffen's journeys up and down the wall had left their mark. In patches you could see right through to the dark red brick. Louis, very damp from his shower, came and looked too.

'We're all going out for pizza in a minute,' he told Abi. 'Theo says the house is too sooty to cook.'

'I know. Why are you putting ivy leaves in your sock?'

'They feel nice.'

Abi looked at him. The leaves were only in his right sock, she noticed, and he was avoiding her eyes.

'You're walking funny,' she told him. 'I noticed earlier.'

'Only in case the leaves fall out.'

Abi frowned, but it was hard to be very worried in broad

146

sunny daylight, with her dad and his friend so pleased with themselves, and Max appearing in a baseball cap he'd got off eBay saying 'I ♥ Paris' on the front and 'Made in China' on the back and Louis so charmed with his nose.

'Now I HAVE to sniff!' he said triumphantly. 'So's not to waste it.'

They had ice cream after the pizza, with strawberry sauce, M&M's, marshmallows and butterscotch chips. Theo's friend said how good he felt to be getting his five a day.

'Five what?' asked Louis.

'Sugar rushes,' he explained. 'I aim for five a day, but I don't always make it. What are you people doing after this, then?'

'Going home to light the fire,' said Abi hopefully, but Theo's friend said, 'I'd stay out of that room for a day or two at least, and leave those sheets hung where they are. That soot's going to be settling for quite a while yet.'

'We should make a list of what we need to do next,' said Theo. 'And we'll have to start thinking about a Christmas tree. First year ever that I've lived in a house with a proper old-fashioned chimney for Santa!'

'A chimney's what you need,' agreed his friend. 'I've never liked leaving the front door unlocked. I mean, I do it. Of course. Cos I want presents . . .'

'I used to try and wait to see him,' said Max.

'I once made a trap out of string across the door,' said Abi. 'And then, when Granny Grace and Dad had gone to sleep, I thought I'd better test it so I got out of bed and just at that moment Dad came in and fell right over and he yelled, "What the heck? What's going on? What were you thinking of, Abi?" and made me take it down.'

'Theo, Theo, Theo,' said his friend, shaking his head. 'Was that reasonable?'

'Yes it was,' said Theo. 'The last thing I needed on my only night off from the annual bloodbath that is A-and-E at Christmas was to be patching up ruddy Santa at two o'clock in the morning!'

'Do you all really truly believe in Santa?' exploded Louis, who had been staring from face to face in increasing astonishment.

'Don't you?' asked Abi.

'NO I DON'T!'

'What *do* you believe in, then?' asked Theo's friend, laughing, and Louis replied at once, 'What you said!'

'What did I say?'

'Magic, or what?' said Louis, and under the table he kicked Abi in conspiracy, while his face shone with such delight that she knew he was thinking of Iffen.

Even so, he camped in Abi's room for a second night, not waiting to be invited, but coming in very clean and a little anxious, and slipping quickly into bed in his socks.

'We need to talk,' said Abi, who had been waiting for him and pounced the moment he arrived.

'I loved Mrs Puddock.'

'Not about Mrs Puddock.'

'Why are you cross?'

'I've seen your leg.'

'When?' squeaked Louis, sounding suddenly alarmed.

'Just before you went into the bathroom, five minutes ago. And when you got into bed. I've been watching. I knew there was something wrong.'

'It's nearly better.'

'Let me look properly.'

Reluctantly, Louis wiggled out of bed and pulled up a pyjama leg to show a deep grey bruise, as big as Abi's hand, with four black holes in it, as if four large nails had caught him there, which they had.

'It wasn't his fault. He whacked the quilt and my leg was underneath.'

'That was *through your quilt?*'

'Ages ago. I put ivy on it to make it better.'

'If it's infected, I'm telling Dad,' said Abi, but it was plain to see that it wasn't. It was a perfect whack by a not quite-real big cat. Heavy, heart-shaped and clean.

'I hope he doesn't miss me while I'm sleeping in here,' said Louis worriedly. 'I left my window open so he didn't scratch the door again, and I put down a bowl of milk.'

'He's not a kitten!'

'I didn't want him to be sad without me.'

'He won't be sad without you.' Abi looked down at Louis' troubled, loving face. 'He'll be off somewhere having adventures. I hope he doesn't meet my foxes.'

'I think he only gets squirrels that are already dead,' said Louis. 'I think he finds them lying under trees.'

'Louis,' said Abi patiently, not arguing with this hopeful opinion, 'what books have you been reading?'

'None,' said Louis, sounding so surprised at this question that Abi knew he was telling the truth. 'None, I promise.'

'You haven't brought home a reading book for days. You'd better not have been dropping them down drains again.'

'I haven't.'

'Where are they, then?'

'I posted them in the letter box by the school gate. To be nice presents for the postman.'

Abi groaned.

'Don't you like the postman? He's very kind! He brings you letters from Granny Grace! I would love him if he brought letters from Granny Grace to me!'

'Please stop talking rubbish and listen to me, Louis!' begged Abi. 'I think Iffen came out of a book.'

'How could he?'

'I don't know, but things do. Remember the snow, and the shell that I found?'

Louis nodded.

'So we need to know which book.'

'Why do we?'

'Louis, he can't stay. He's getting more and more dangerous.'

Louis' face crumpled.

'Do you know what he'd be doing, in his real life? He'd be hunting. Goats, perhaps, or wild pigs. Deer, for sure. Crouching in the long grass, watching the herds race past. The sunshine and shadows all mixed up in dapples on his spotty coat, so he's nearly invisible. Out in the wild, where he used to be.'

'Did Iffen use to be out in the wild?'

'Yes.'

'Not in London?'

'No.'

'Which do you think he likes best?'

'Which do *you* think he likes best?'

'Not here,' said Louis sadly, and turned away. Abi watched his shoulders move, shakily at first, and then more slowly and steadily as his snuffles stopped, and all the while she thought, *Which book? Which book? Which book?*

But it was Max who found the book.

CHAPTER SIXTEEN

Sunday morning began early with Theo being called into work. He had shouted the news to the family upstairs, made an emergency phone call, and rushed out to collect Esmé in Polly's old car. Before anyone was up she was being unloaded on the doorstep, laden with books and art materials.

'You are an angel,' Theo told her.

'I charge extra three pounds an hour for Sunday,' said Esmé, smiling angelically.

'Bargain!' said Theo, and was gone.

The arrival of Esmé got them all out of bed. Abi wrapped herself in her dressing gown and went down to say hello. Max took over the bathroom, cleaned his teeth twice and practised, '*Bon jour! Ça va? Très cool to voir you*,' in the shower. Louis wandered, shivering and sleepy, down to his bedroom in search of his clothes and found he couldn't open the door.

He pushed and pushed and it was like pushing a wall. It didn't move a millimetre.

He lay on the floor and tried to look under the gap at the bottom, but there was nothing to be seen except darkness.

He joggled the door handle.

Nothing.

Louis lay back down again and prodded under the door with an ivy leaf from out of his sock. There was something there; he could feel it.

'Iffen,' breathed Louis through the keyhole.

There was no reply and Louis knew why. It was because he, Louis, had deserted his friend. Needed him, loved him and then deserted him.

'Iffen, I'm coming,' he whispered, and then crept downstairs and outside in his pyjamas. He hesitated, dancing from foot to foot on the damp ground beneath his bedroom window, and then began to climb the ivy. At first he managed quickly, finding handholds and toeholds easily amongst the knotty stems. He moved higher and higher, until he reached the overhang of his bedroom windowsill.

Where he stuck.

All in a moment, Louis had gone from not frightened at all to frozen with fear. Now his feet refused to move and his fingers would not unclamp. For a long time he hung there, like a small pyjama-clad starfish plastered against the leaves, first not looking down, and then looking down, which was terrible. *Wobble, wobble, wobble*, went Louis' bottom lip, and he cried wet tears on to the dark green ivy.

In the kitchen Abi ate toast and honey, Esmé spread her drawing book over more than half the table and Max appeared, smelling very strongly of a variety of products that he had acquired at school from the PE lost-property crate. They all had exotic, untamed names like Lynx and Savanna and Urban Rebel and Wild, Wild, Wild.

'*Ouf!*' said Esmé, sneezing.

'*Bonjour,*' said Max, only slightly put off. '*Ça va?*' he continued, waving his arms about like he assumed French people did. '*Très* . . . What's the matter?'

'Everything is good,' said Esmé, sneezing again, and she ducked firmly back into her book and was lost.

Max abandoned his French and said, 'I'm having some cereal,' in a rather cross voice, as if someone had said that he couldn't. Abi made coffee, enough for all three of them, and Max mellowed a bit at that. It wasn't until they'd drunk it, and searched the fridge for yoghurt, and found the TV remote in with the salad, and switched on and off several cartoons and the news, that anyone asked, 'Where's Louis?'

Then, after a bit of calling and hunting, they discovered that his bedroom door was jammed.

'He's wedged it,' said Max, and shouted, 'Oi, Louis! Open up!'

At first they heard nothing, but when Max tried again, Louis' voice came quavering back from far, far away, much further than the other side of the door, 'I'mstuckontheivy!'

'What?' they called, one after another.

'Stuck!' replied Louis.

'Stuck?'

'*Où es tu*, Louis?' called Esmé.

155

'On the IVY!' wailed Louis in reply, and with that Abi and Max and Esmé all raced down the stairs and out of the front door and round the house, staring upwards at the walls, and there, sure enough, was Louis, stuck on the ivy below his bedroom window.

'Louis, you mad kid!' exclaimed Max, while Abi exclaimed, 'Cushions!' and sprinted back inside. She and Esmé collected an armload each and returned to find Max already climbing.

'Be careful!' begged Louis.

'*Me* be careful?' repeated Max, already quite far off the ground, elbow deep in leaves, searching for handholds. He was climbing well to the side of Louis, so as not to put weight on ivy that his little brother might be holding, digging his toes into crevices, and dislodging dust and leaves with each step.

'I'm going to fall!' whimpered Louis.

'No, you're not,' said Max. 'Keep still! Don't twist round to look at me! I can nearly touch your foot! Whoa!'

Abi gasped. Esmé covered her mouth with both hands. A whole huge stem of ivy detached and swung down from the wall.

Max dropped two metres, and for a moment or two, hung by one hand.

Louis gave a sob.

'Shut up, I'm fine!' growled Max. He launched himself sideways and upwards, attached himself to the wall again, and carried on until he could call to Louis, 'I'm right underneath you. Hold tight to the windowsill, and then you've got to sit down on my shoulders.'

'I don't want to.'

'Tough. Get on with it. Lower yourself slowly . . . Now, let go with one hand and grab on to some ivy . . . Now the other . . .'

Below, Abi and Esmé anxiously rearranged cushions.

'OK, now we're going down like a ladder,' Max told Louis. 'Keep holding the ivy to balance. Your knees are flipping bony! You needn't grip on so tight.'

He lowered himself carefully, foothold by foothold.

'Halfway!' called Abi, a few minutes later. 'Well done, Louis!'

'Well done, *Louis*?' demanded Max. 'Wow, this ivy is loose! Get out of the way in case I have to jump!'

'Jump?' squeaked Louis, letting go of the ivy and grabbing two handfuls of hair instead.

'OW!' yelled Max, and skidded vertically downwards in a shower of leaves.

Esmé grabbed Louis, just in time to stop him tumbling. Max leaped the last stretch. Abi exclaimed, 'Brilliant! Brilliant!' and Louis said, 'Thank you, Max, thank you, thank you!' and hugged him.

''S OK,' said Max, unused to being treated like a superhero, and stomped into the kitchen to finish his breakfast.

As soon as Louis was back in the house, he bolted upstairs, with Abi behind. This meant that Max was left alone with Esmé, and for once she was smiling and looking at him. To cover his sudden awareness of this frightening and yet

157

wonderful situation, he pulled her art book his way and began studying the pages.

Some were collages: notes in French, tiny colour blocks, photographs, and maps copied out of books. Others were huge double pages, entirely filled with sketches of animals. Max paused at a great herd of bison racing across two full pages. As he stared at them, trying to fathom their distant, unfamiliar power, he was aware of Esmé just behind him, not sneezing now, or saying, '*Ouf!*', just standing quietly as he looked at her work.

Presently she said, 'You did so good, Max, helping Louis,' and leaned over and picked a stray ivy leaf out of his hair. '*Très cool*,' she added, with a laugh in her voice as she tucked it behind her ear. '*Très cool*,' and she pressed the back of his neck very gently, with two warm fingers. Very lightly, and only for a moment, but enough that Max knew then, once and forever, that there was such a thing as magic. For down into the dizzying deepness of time slid Max, leaving everything behind except the echo of Esmé's fingers like two warm prints upon his skin. And although he could not look up, could only stare into the book and feel the strange shaking of his heart, he gradually became aware that a warm new world was opening all around him.

Max found he could raise his head and there was sunlight. His senses filled with summer: a dry grass and chalk smell, the glare of ultraviolet, bees humming, crickets whirring and a rumbling dust cloud coming closer and closer. Bison, twenty or thirty at least, with lighter coloured young ones galloping beside. In a moment they were pounding past, so close that in a few steps he could have reached out and touched them. They were dark shapes, and brown flanks, curved horns and snorting muzzles, racing down a sunlit valley. Behind them, nothing more than faded golden shadows in the dust cloud, a glimpse of two pursuers, leaping cat shapes.

They were gone.

Max bent and touched the ground, and it was gritty and real. The grasses were waist height, thin and yellow where he stood, greener under the shadow of the white chalk cliffs. Overhead, as the dust cleared, was pale, achingly blue sky, where half a dozen hawks rose in lazy spirals on the thermals. There was no wind. The crickets, or whatever they were, grew electric shrill. Gradually he realized that he was standing on a track of beaten earth and he turned to see it rising upwards towards the cliffs.

The heat was dizzying.

'*Très cool*,' said Esmé, very clearly. 'So.'

The summer colours faded, sunlight withdrew and the sounds diminished. He was back in his own world again.

'So,' repeated Esmé, reaching for her book. 'What a morning!'

He stared at her, speechless.

'You saw?'

Max nodded, and knew then without her saying, that whatever he had seen, Esmé had seen too. Perhaps many times. How else had she drawn those pictures?

He shook his buzzing head, but his thoughts would not untangle themselves.

'You OK, Max?'

'Oh yes,' said Max huskily. 'Yes. Oh yes. Yes.'

'Louis should come down and eat breakfast.'

'What?'

'Food. For Louis.'

Max nodded. She wasn't making sense, but he thought he'd better agree.

'Please, Max, go and fetch Louis, because Theo said, "See Louis eats,"' said Esmé patiently, and this penetrated and Max knew where he was and jumped to his feet and then paused.

Esmé was already at work on a new page, her smooth dark head bent, her slim brown hands busy with charcoal and crayon, but she looked up when he asked, 'Esmé, how long ago?'

'Louis? Ten minutes, more, since he went up with Abi.'

'Not Louis. These pictures you draw. How long ago, when they were drawn the first time?'

'Ah,' said Esmé. 'I think maybe you say thirty thousand years?'

'Thirty . . . Those animals running? Those . . . What is that you're drawing now?'

'*Ours*, bear,' said Esmé.

'There were *bears*?'

'Bears, yes, bison. Horses, deer. Cats, hyena, *rhinocéros* . . .'

'*Rhinoceros!*' Max rubbed his eyes, and his hands were dusty, his jeans, his shirt, his arms, all white with dust. 'And it was *thirty thousand* . . .'

'Years,' finished Esmé. '*Oui.*'

CHAPTER SEVENTEEN

Meanwhile, upstairs, nothing had changed. Louis' bedroom door was still immovable.

'Help me push!' he begged Abi, but Abi wouldn't. Whatever Iffen was, she thought – green magic, illusion, dappled prowler of unknown pages – he was, most of all, a creature that shouldn't be pushed.

'Leave him!' she told Louis. 'Let him go when he's ready. Come down to the kitchen with Esmé and me.'

'I can't. He might need me!' said Louis, once more on the floor peering into the dark. 'He might be trapped!'

'Nothing could trap Iffen!'

'Well then, he might be dead!'

'Who might be dead?' asked Max, coming up the stairs behind them.

Louis didn't reply. Instead he scrambled to his feet and launched himself at the door one last time. This time it flew open as if no weight had ever held it. It flew wide open, so that Max clearly saw a huge spotted cat spring lightly on to Louis' bed, pause to glare over its shoulder, spit out an indignant '*Tcha!*' and take a great curving leap through the window.

'What was that? What the heck was that?' screeched Max, rushing into the room. 'LOUIS! Answer me! What was that just then?'

'Iffen,' said Louis, as calmly as Esmé had said, a few minutes before, '*Rhinocéros*'.

'Iffen? Iffen?' repeated Max, now hanging out of the window. 'What d'you mean, Iffen?'

'That's his name.'

'Did you know it was there? Have you seen it before? Crikey, Louis!'

'Max, he's not real,' said Abi.

'What do you mean? I don't know what you mean! He looked bloody real to me! Aren't you bothered that something the size of a . . . of a . . . LION just shot out of my brother's bedroom window?'

'Course I am.'

'Where's it gone?'

'I don't know.'

'Well, where'd it come from?'

'Out of a book, I think.'

'You're mad. You're both mad,' said Max, staring. At the window, at Abi and Louis, at the place where Iffen had been. And then, without quite knowing why, at the white dust fading his black jeans to grey, his red sweatshirt to pinkish . . .

'I'm going to ring the police before that thing kills someone,' he said, but he spoke much less certainly than he had a moment before. His panic had passed. He didn't know what to think, hadn't really known what to think since Esmé's warm touch on the back of his neck.

'Just tell me what's going on,' he begged, and allowed his spine to slump against the bedroom wall, and then to slide down until he was sitting on the floor, with his knees hunched, and his eyes closed, and the bumping of his heart gradually slowing.

'You couldn't see him before,' said Louis. 'Neither could I, because it was dark and I wanted a nowl. I could see his ears, but nowls have them too sometimes – ask Abi. He's been coming for ages, bigger and bigger. Sometimes with squirrels. Dead.'

Louis stopped and looked expectantly at Max, as if to say, *I have explained everything. Be pleased.*

Max banged his head against the wall to see if he was in the middle of a mad, jumbled nightmare, but he didn't wake up into a fresh, sane world, so he knew he wasn't. He could smell crushed ivy. The window was still open. He had been to a place where Esmé said there were rhinoceroses and there were definitely bison and whatever was chasing them; he knew, because he'd seen them himself. He was covered in incomprehensible white dust. He closed his eyes again. Abi was talking.

A balsa-wood raft on the Pacific Ocean. An attic in Amsterdam, and horse-chestnut leaves. The lurch of the bus. She was talking about books. Usually she just read them, and never said a word. But now she was saying really weird things about books and a blizzard . . .

Max opened his eyes and looked at her.

'It was like a dream,' she said. 'One moment I was here in the house, the next I was there. I know it's impossible. It doesn't happen always. You have to be reading . . .' Abi paused, and glanced at Max, expecting to be called insane, but his eyes were looking at her almost as if he understood. 'You have to be reading . . . deeply . . . with all of you . . .' she said. 'You know, how you read so everything else goes away . . . ?'

Max nodded.

'On the raft I slipped and dropped my book and a wave splashed over it. It's still a bit damp. It tastes of salt. Later there was white sand. Hot white sand, and I picked up a shell. Another time it happened when I was just looking at a picture.'

'Yes,' said Max.

'You're there, in the book world, and then, without choosing, you're not. You hear a voice, and it calls you back. You called me back from the bus, Max. Louis called me out of the blizzard.'

'Esmé called me,' said Max. 'From . . . I don't know what from. She said thirty thousand years.'

Max still couldn't make any sense of those thirty thousand years.

'It's happened to you too?' asked Abi, and was surprised at the sudden jealousy that hit her. Yet another private world to be shared.

'Just now,' Max said, and described the racing herd, the cricket-screeching valley with the white chalk cliffs, the dust that had billowed. He said, 'Look, I'm still covered,' and showed them, and he was.

'I'll show you Abi's shell,' said Louis suddenly, and, without asking if he could, raced up to Abi's room and fetched it. He plonked it down in front of Max, who instead of picking it up looked at Abi and asked, 'Do you mind?'

Third time's the charm, Granny Grace used to say, *and then the change.*

Max had made the rocking-horse joke. He had said, *This can be Abi's room, because of the books.* Now, for a third time, he had warmed her heart with his hesitant *Do you mind?*

Abi's jealousy left her like a bond untying and she saw the true Max behind the wary eyes. The fellow traveller. Her relief was like lightness. Max would help.

'Abi had snow, too, but it melted,' said Louis. 'Now do you understand about Iffen?'

'Tell me again.'

The second time was easier for Max. He began to grasp even the nowls that his little brother had tried to tempt to his window. He managed not to be distracted by the pigeon that didn't fly. Despite the fact that Louis could not sit still and talk of Iffen – had to flap his arms like nowls, hold his hands above his tatty head for ears, bounce on and off his bed, reach out of the window for ivy leaves – Max followed, from the first glimpse of dappled fur, the glorious story of Iffen and how he grew.

He listened to it all.

Then Louis stopped. He turned his head away because to speak on felt like betrayal. It was Abi who showed Max the patchwork mat and commanded Louis to roll down his sock and lift the ivy leaves.

'I'm worried now,' said Abi.

Louis sat very close to Max and held a fistful of the dusty sweatshirt tight, so that he could not leave until he had heard more. How the bruise had been an accident, that he had been under the quilt and Iffen hadn't meant to do it, and that it didn't hurt. But even as the words tumbled around him, Louis saw the growing alarm on Max's face, saw his eyes on Abi's, and watched as they spoke to each other without words.

He guessed that Max was agreeing with what Abi had said the night before. That this was no world for Iffen, and that he couldn't stay.

'*À bientôt!*'

They all jumped.

It was Esmé calling from the doorstep. The morning had flown away over their heads. They raced for the stairs, but the front door slammed and she was gone. Only an ivy leaf left in the hall, dropped from her hair as she hurried. Max picked it up and folded it into his empty wallet. He thought he would keep it forever.

Then Theo and his bike came clattering into the house. Theo was pleased with himself. There were people recovering who might not have been if he hadn't rushed off so quickly, and now he was full of plans. They were going to roast potatoes and onions and stuffing balls and veggie sausages, and there would be baked tomatoes and a sticky toffee pudding he'd bought on the way home. Proper Sunday lunch, as fast as they could make it.

'Couldn't Esmé have stayed too?' Abi asked, and Theo said he'd asked, but she'd been in a hurry. She'd rushed away the moment she saw him ride up on his bike.

'She's left her book that she draws in,' remarked Louis, and so she had. Her huge portfolio, as big as a desk, was still on the kitchen table.

'Better put it somewhere safe,' said Theo, and Max took it to the rocking-horse room where he could not resist looking inside once again.

Les Artistes et les Animaux de la grotte Chauvet

'The Artists and Animals of the Chauvet Cave,' Max read, on what Esmé had made into a title page, above a drawing of a huge branching map. Turning the heavy grey pages, Max found his running bison, and then deer in herds. There were more of Louis' handprints, in ochre red and black and grey. He discovered the profile of an enormous bear. Rhinoceros and hyenas. Horses and horses, galloping, tossing their heads, horses overlaid with horses. Strange markings too, scored lines like arrowheads, swirling curves of finger traces, and then mammoths, an owl, two reindeer, feline shapes . . .

Feline shapes?

'Max!' The door swung open, and there was Esmé, out of

breath. 'You have it!' she exclaimed, and seized it from his hands.

'Could I just . . .'

'No, no, I have to hand it in!'

'Hand it in?'

'End of assignment, hand it in. Tomorrow.'

'Please, Esmé, could you leave it here, just for one night?'

'*Non, non!* Why should I? *Mais non!*'

'So I can show Louis.'

'Louis has seen it many times. I must go. *À bientôt*, Max!'

That night, when Polly called to tell them not to forget their PE kit, and to ask what they'd had for supper, and to check that homework had been done and school bags packed for morning, Louis asked her when she was coming home. There was a very small, tiny, minute moment of pause, between Louis finishing speaking and Polly saying, 'Very, very soon, Louis!'

'You'd forgotten!' said Louis, accusingly. 'You'd forgotten all about coming home!' and he flung away the phone and launched a blubbering attack on Theo because it was clearly all his fault.

Theo took a deep breath, scooped up Louis and hugged him tight, and said, 'Time we talked about Christmas. What'll we get for Polly, everyone? Abi? Max? Help me out! Who's got some good ideas?'

Max tried. He remembered that Polly liked black-and-white films, and that once he'd bought her chocolates with cherries in and she'd said they were her favourite. Abi said sparkly earrings were Christmassy. Theo said he'd seen a pink-and-gold scarf and very nearly bought it, only he thought he'd ask them first. 'Shall I buy it?' he asked Louis, and Louis gave a small nod. 'All right, I will!' said Theo, and then ruined all their good work by saying cheerfully, 'And what about Mrs P.?'

'She's gone away! You know she has!' cried Louis, and began howling when they laughed, and said horrible Abi had taken Mrs Puddock away, and he'd never camp in her room again. Abi was awful and so was Max, and Theo was the worst, and he wanted Iffen.

'Iffen?' Theo asked with his eyebrows raised, and Abi murmured uncomfortably that Iffen was sort of a story.

'Iffen is real!' said Louis, now completely losing his temper. 'You *saw* he was real!' and he lunged at Abi, and missed.

'There's quite a moon tonight,' remarked Theo, and took Louis out into the cool night air to look at it and afterwards straight up to his room. There he sat on the floor and began a lot of talk about rockets and space; how astronauts went to the loo, what they ate, and how they managed not to float out of bed. Theo's monologue on space travel had bored many a frantic child to stillness in the past. He had it down to perfection: the quiet, slow words, the floating teaspoons, the unsurprising views that drifted past the rocket's steamed-up portholes. Louis yawned and yawned and was asleep within minutes of touching down on his pillow, with his quilt round his ears, his window tight shut, and his bedroom door ajar in case he should need to call for comfort in the night.

Not long afterwards, Theo was also sleeping the easy sleep of the heroic and exhausted, but Max and Abi were not. They hovered uncomfortably on the attic stairs.

'I can't go to bed,' whispered Abi, 'not with Iffen out there and Louis on his own, even if the window's shut.'

'Louis' window wouldn't stop a thing that size,' said Max. 'It's not even double glazed – it could knock it out with one swipe. The minute we hear something, you drag Theo awake and I'll charge the room.'

'We'll both charge the room. We'll yell to Dad on the way.'

'I've been thinking about where it's come from.'

'Iffen?'

'Yes. And everything. I don't know what's been going on.'

'Green magic,' said Abi. 'That's what Granny Grace said. Shush now. We've got to listen.'

The night was soundless. Unbearably quiet. Silence rang in their minds like bells. At midnight Abi said she didn't know how she was going to manage school in the morning, and at one o'clock Max suggested they take turns to stay awake. At half past one they brought their pillows and quilts out on to the stairs. Stairs made a sufficiently uncomfortable bed to allow them to believe they could safely close their eyes.

They did.

About five in the morning one of them slid into the other and the bump woke them up. They could hear large bearish snores from Theo, and small bearish snuffles from Louis, and nothing else, not an ivy leaf moving. The house had become very cold.

'I've had enough,' said Max. 'This is stupid. It's nearly morning and it's freezing. I'm going to check he's OK and then I'm going to bed.'

Abi nodded, too tired to argue. 'Be careful. We mustn't wake him,' she murmured as she followed after Max.

'We won't.'

Louis' door was still ajar. Very gently Max pushed it further, stepped softly on to the patchwork rug, smelt greenness and December air, realized with horror that the window was now wide open, and froze.

Louis looked like prey.

Prey caught between two giant paws. Limp. His pillow slipped sideways, his quilt thrown back and Iffen's head raised above him, Iffen's eyes watching, Iffen's shoulder blades sharp, outlined against the dark of the window, and his haunches crouched into a waiting spring.

Max felt his stomach churn with fear.

Abi, one step behind him, shrieked out loud.

Iffen's ears went flat against his head, his lips curled back, and at the same time, across the landing, the large bear snores stopped and were replaced by great heavings and growls and suddenly Theo was amongst them.

'I don't believe it!' Theo groaned, pushing past them both, 'Whatever's going on? Is someone ill? Who opened that window?'

Louis, with his eyes tight shut, murmured, 'I did. Go away. It isn't morning,' and reached out to Iffen. Max exclaimed, 'Theo, can't you *see*?'

Iffen snarled silently, head low, neck arched into a crest, the light from the landing reflecting curved lines of brightness down ivory-coloured fangs.

Abi begged, 'Dad! Get Louis! Quick!'

Theo glanced at her as if she were mad, murmured, 'What's the matter with you?' tugged the quilt from between Iffen's two massive front paws to tuck it round Louis' shoulders, and said, 'I'm going to close that window!'

'No!' wailed Louis, pushing him away. 'I don' wan' it shut! Go away, leave me alone!'

'OK, OK, Louis, I'll leave it,' whispered Theo. 'Just didn't want you cold.'

'I'm hot!' said Louis, and rolled over, deep into Iffen's chest.

'Right!' said Theo to Max and Abi. 'He's fine. He's asleep again. Now, you two, bed!'

He turned Abi round, ushered Max out of the door, and said, 'I don't know what you were thinking of. Poor little kid, creeping in on him like that. Get back to sleep, the pair of you!'

'We can't leave Louis in there!' said Abi.

'Bed,' said Theo, terribly, on guard at Louis' door.

'Will you stay with him?' asked Max. 'Because I'm not going anywhere if—'

'Listen!' interrupted Abi.

Outside, the ivy stirred suddenly, as if a wind had passed through it. The green smell became strong again. There came a quiet, heavy thump. Abi ducked under Theo's arm to check if what she thought had happened was true, and it was.

'Gone!' she told Max.

'I am losing patience,' said Theo, who never lost patience, so they retreated back up the attic stairs. There they waited, hidden in shadows, and saw Theo peep round at Louis, saw his face melt to a smile, watched him cross the landing to his own room.

In an incredibly short time, the large bear snore and the small bear snuffle resumed again. However, the night wasn't over for Abi and Max. Louis' window was still open. They gathered their discarded quilts around them, and settled down on the attic stairs to wait it out till morning.

'Esmé's art book,' whispered Max.

'What?'

'That's where he's from. Her cave art. All those animals.'

'Of course!' exclaimed Abi, as soon as she understood. 'Of course! Of course he is! And Louis has seen it loads of times! Max, tonight, when she brings it . . .'

'She's handing it in today.'

'She can't!'

'She told me yesterday.'

'He's got to go back, Max. He's too big. He's *much* too big. Louis knows he is too.'

'At least we know where he's from now. When I . . . when that weird thing happened to me, after I got Louis down off the wall – I told you – and I was covered in that white dust?'

'Yes?'

'There was something chasing those bison. Big cats, a bit like Louis', not spotted, but big like Iffen.'

'I'll text Esmé when it's properly morning,' said Abi. 'I'll try and explain. I'll ask if we can borrow it, just for a little while. Maybe she could give it in late.'

'Even if we had it, what could we do?'

'I don't know yet. Something. It must be the way.'

'I think so.'

'I'll get it. I'll explain everything. She'll probably think we're mad.'

'Doesn't matter. Anything.'

'Anything,' Abi agreed.

Morning came and it was awful. A winter gale blew through the house from Louis' open window. Abi and Max felt sick from lack of sleep. Theo texted Polly an unhappy message: Home Sweet Home?

I hope so, Polly wrote back.

CHAPTER EIGHTEEN

It was lunchtime, and Max was lurking by the bike shelter. It was one of the two places where it was possible to avoid the school's mobile-phone signal blocker. Max knew that Danny must be balanced on a toilet seat, hanging out of a top-floor washroom window, because that was the other place. Danny was busy sending his customary daily insults. Experience had taught Max that if he didn't pay attention to them when they first arrived, they would be shouted to him in public half an hour later, so he was replying back as best he could, which wasn't very well. He was so sleepy he could hardly think, and everything was extra complicated because Abi was messaging him too.

Abi had not been able to contact Esmé all morning. At lunchtime she sent a frantic plea to Max: She isn't answering me. You'll have to go into the art college and find her.

The art college was close to school, but that didn't help much. You couldn't just walk in. You had to go through reception and get a visitor's pass. Max knew this from Danny, who always had to ask for one if he wanted a lift home with his mum.

I'm not sure I can do that, Max texted back.

MAX, replied Abi, seconds later, in panicking capitals. YOU SAW IFFEN LAST NIGHT WITH LOUIS. THINK OF SOMETHING!

Wait, wrote Max. Give me a minute.

A moment later his phone pinged again and this time it was Danny. A long one. *I can't read it now. I'll answer Abi first,* thought Max.

Sorry, sorry, he wrote hurriedly to Abi. I have been thinking. Talk soon. OK?

Then he turned to Danny's latest.

> On the third day of Christmas Santa sent to me
> Three French snogs
> From my babysitter
> Cos I am her Santa babeeeeeee

It wasn't really up to his friend's usual standard of rudeness, but Max supposed it was hard to think of something fresh every day. *Poor old Danny,* he thought.

And, *I hope he doesn't start singing that.*

And, *If I hadn't picked him up . . .*

More than anything, almost, Max wished he hadn't picked Danny up.

But he had. He'd done it. He'd made a joke about Danny's worst thing; Danny, who when he was ten years old had wanted to grow so much he hung from the top of his bedroom door and begged Max, 'Pull really hard on my feet!'

They'd kept it up for weeks, the hanging, and pulling, and the scribble of marks on the door where Max had measured him afterwards. The marks had crawled up, millimetre by millimetre, and then, devastatingly, down again. Danny had been so frightened at this measurable shrinking that on Max's advice ('They'll give you hormones or something') he'd told his mum and she'd taken him to the doctor's. Danny had told the doctor about the hanging and the measurements and then asked bravely, 'Can't you give me hormones or something?'

The doctor had stood up and looked out of the window. His shoulders shook.

He'd said, 'Your dad's normal height, your mum is too. Your brothers are all fine. You're taller than the last time I saw you. I can't give you hormones for a wrecked bedroom door.'

'What?'

'You're not shrinking. Your door's sagging. You've pulled it off its hinges.'

At this wonderful sanity Danny had bolted from the doctor's and run all the way home, and it was true. The screws on the hinges were hardly holding the door to the frame. He had hugged Max, jubilant.

Not long afterwards they had started their bike-repair and car-cleaning business.

They had been such friends.

Max looked at Danny's latest message. He was so tired he

couldn't think of a single rude remark to send back. He didn't want to anyway. He was weary with it all.

MAX?? texted Abi, and Max's thoughts turned back to her, and the unbelievable problem of the Stone Age spotted cat conjured by Louis from Esmé's soon-to-vanish art portfolio.

Simultaneously, Danny came running towards him.

Danny was waving his battered mobile phone high in the air and his face was shining with happiness. 'I got your text!' he called, skidding to a halt in front of Max. 'Thanks for saying sorry! Thanks for saying you'd talk! How's it going, Maxi-babe?'

'I . . .' began Max, glancing down at his list of sent messages, and realizing what had happened. He'd got muddled. He'd said sorry to Danny by mistake.

Suddenly he was very glad.

'I've been sorry for ages,' he said truthfully. 'And it's not going perfectly, actually.'

Danny's mouth fell open with surprise.

'Not perfect with Esmé?'

'Not anything with Esmé,' said Max. 'I wish! She hardly knows I exist.'

'Mate,' said Danny, completely stunned by this honesty. 'That's rubbish.'

'Yes, well,' said Max. 'A lot of things have been rubbish lately.'

'A lot of things?'

'Yep.'

'Did something else happen besides me?'

178

The thought of explaining to Danny what else had happened besides him, complete with mythical beasts, ripped rugs, Stone Age cave art, ivy and sitting on the stairs all night, was so impossible that Max could only nod his head.

'Maybe I can help!' suggested Danny. 'I mean, not with Esmé of course, but with anything else . . .'

'It's Esmé I need help with, though, Dan.'

'Mate,' began Danny, deeply shaken and feeling like his own grandma. 'Mate, she's . . . I mean . . . French. And eighteen . . . You may be a bit out of your league, mate . . .' His grandma's words would have been '*all going to end in tears*'.

He bravely said them.

'You don't understand,' said Max.

'I do, I do. All my brothers, one time or another, I've seen them on their knees . . .'

'I'm not on my knees!' said Max. 'Not at all! Anyway, eighteen . . . it's not like she's twenty or something. I'll be nearly sixteen myself next year . . .'

Danny, who was good at maths, looked surprised, but did not argue and instead said, 'Course you will. Nearly. More or less. About.'

'I've got to see her,' said Max.

'You have?'

'Yes, and really quickly. Now. About her art.'

Danny looked at him in disbelief. Max saw the look and explained a bit more.

'You know those great big art books they do? She's been

doing hers at our house and there's something come out of it that needs to go back in.'

'Like a painting or something?' asked Danny. 'One of the pages come loose?'

'Yeah, sort of,' said Max, picturing Iffen. 'Yeah, there's something got loose, that's right. And she's handing her book in today, so I've got to stop her.'

'Can't you just message her or something?' asked Danny, not believing a word of it.

'She's not answering.'

'Does it matter that much? One loose page?'

'It isn't just one loose page.'

'How many?'

'I can't explain, Danny,' said Max a bit desperately. 'I just need to see her, that's all.'

'Mate, you've got it bad!' said Danny. 'OK! Tell you what, straight after last lesson, soon as we can, we'll go over to the college. I'll say I need to see my mum to get a lift home, and you're coming with me. Soon as they sign us in you can shoot off and find her.'

'Thanks, Danny,' said Max gratefully. 'Thanks, really, really thanks! Thank you! Oh . . .'

It was another message from Abi: You've had a minute. You've had ages!

Thought of something, Max sent back. Danny's helping.

It's got to work, wrote Abi to Max.

'It's got to work,' said Max to Danny.

180

'Trust me!' said Danny, happier than he'd been for weeks. 'It will.'

At first it didn't seem like it would. They reached the college, breathless from running, and were signed in at reception by someone who knew Danny's four brothers and wanted a good long chat about each of them. It seemed hours until they escaped at last into the teeming corridors. There Max glimpsed Esmé, lost her, raced, caught up with her again and found himself mistaken.

'Esmé?' asked the stranger. 'Never heard of her.'

'She's French, you must have,' said Danny, who had come panting up behind.

The stranger rolled unfriendly eyes, sighed and walked away.

'What'll we do?' asked Max, despairing, and just then Danny's mother arrived.

'Danny! Max!' she exclaimed. 'Just who I need! Follow me, follow me, follow me!' And she rushed them into an office at the back of a big messy classroom. 'Hold out your arms!' she ordered, and loaded half a huge pile of art portfolios into Danny's, the other half into Max's, and added her keys to Danny's heap. 'Find my car and plonk them in the boot!' she told them. 'You've dropped something, Max, I'll get it for you! There!'

Then she rushed away again.

Max did not move. He stood and stared. There, in his arms, was Esmé's portfolio, with the ivy leaf that had fallen from her hair on the top.

It was fate, it was green magic, helping him out at last. Max dumped his armload, retrieved the ivy leaf, picked up Esmé's book, and said, 'Dan, I'm taking this and running!'

'Why?' asked Danny. 'What about seeing Esmé? I thought the whole point of coming here . . .'

'Cover for me, will you? I'll bring it back as soon as I can.'

'Mate, you know you're not making sense any more?'

Danny found that he was talking to himself. Max was gone. 'Maxi-babe,' he said, shaking his head, then gathered up the whole great heap of portfolios and staggered very slowly to the car park.

On the way back to look for his mum, he walked right into Esmé.

Esmé stumbled a bit.

'*Pardon!*' said Danny, blushing. 'Sorry, Esmé!'

Esmé's eyes narrowed and she asked, 'Do I know you?'

'*Non,*' said Danny. 'But I know you *parce que* – you babysit my friend Max.'

'I do?'

'You must have noticed Max!'

'What you mean, noticed?' asked Esmé, yawning politely behind a slim brown hand.

'Noticed . . . er . . . observed, detected, clocked, checked out, taken in . . . um . . . considered or regarded,' offered Danny, who was excellent at English, as well as French and maths.

'Regarded?' asked Esmé, and then suddenly she smiled, glancing at Danny in such a way that for a moment he felt his knees become as unreliable as ever any of his brothers' had.

Crikey! he thought, reaching out for a wall to steady himself. *Crikey, poor Max!*

'*Quoi pauvre Max?*' asked Esmé, and Danny realized that he had spoken aloud. 'I take care of his brother, Louis, *mais bien sûr, j'ai remarqué Max!*'

'She said something about Louis,' Danny said, ages later, trying to recall it all for his friend. 'And then she said something about you.'

'What did she say?'

'She said, "*Mais bien sûr, j'ai remarqué Max.*"'

Danny paused, and looked expectantly at his friend.

'Come on,' said Max. 'What's it mean? You're the one who went to Disneyland, not me!'

'It means,' said Danny, '"But of course I have noticed Max"!'

'She said that? She really said that?'

'Yep,' said Danny, 'she did.'

CHAPTER NINETEEN

Most days, Louis went to his After-school Club until Esmé arrived to collect him. It was a club that liked parties. They had celebrated Diwali with sweets and lanterns, and Hanukkah with games and gold-and-silver chocolate money, and now they were getting ready for Christmas. They were making Christmas decorations to hang on the school tree: red-and-white woven paper hearts, fat felt robins, gingerbread stars and cotton-wool lambs.

'Lambs?' asked Louis, and they showed him the Christmas crib set up on the windowsill, with the stable and the star, the manger and the baby, the Three Wise Men and the shepherd boy, and his flock of snow-white lambs.

'Okay, lambs,' said Louis, nodding.

Louis' lamb did not look like the other children's. It was a strange, sinewy beast, with pointed ears and teeth. It came in for a lot of criticism.

'Its tail is too long,' said Lucy.

'Lambs don't have spots,' said Jay.

'It doesn't look like a lamb at all,' said Amit, which was

perfectly true. It didn't look like a lamb; it looked like a giant spotted cat, big enough to eat all the lambs on the Christmas tree, with the robins for pudding afterwards.

Summer (who always had dreadful colds in winter) sneezed and said it wasn't very nice. Summer's family didn't celebrate Diwali or Hanukkah or Christmas. Summer was waiting for December Solstice Day, when there would be sweets and candles and a chocolate Yule log and piles of presents under a tree strung with lights. 'With a picture of me on the top,' said Summer proudly.

'Yuck,' said Amit.

Summer's lamb was white and fat and cotton-wool fluffy. Summer poked Louis' lamb-that-wasn't-a-lamb and said it looked dirty.

'He's meant to be that colour,' said Louis. 'And he's meant to have spots. And his tail isn't too long either.'

'It's a monster-lamb,' said Summer, and she waved her hand in the air to attract one of the After-school Club supervisors and said, 'Miss, look! Louis has made a monster-lamb!'

'Perhaps you'd like to try again, Louis,' said the supervisor in a kind, tired voice.

Louis shook his head.

'Cut off its tail,' urged Amit.

'You shouldn't have done teeth,' said Lucy.

'It could be a black lamb,' suggested Jay, 'if you blobbed all the spots together.'

'It would still be monster, though,' said Summer. 'Miss, Louis is crying!'

Louis picked up his lamb-that-wasn't-a-lamb, grabbed his jacket from the back of his chair, shoved past Summer, dodged Amit, pushed away one supervisor, stepped over the other (who was half under a table picking up spilt googly eyes), made it to the door and ran. He ran along a corridor and across the back of the hall, where a recorder club was tormenting a Christmas carol to shrieking ribbons, past the office where someone lay on a plastic sofa hugging a bucket, and out of the playground door, wading against the flow of the Eights-and-over Football Team, who were just now streaming in. The footballers covered his tracks long enough for him to reach the gate. Then he was out in the wild, the true wild, where he was never allowed alone, the city street at the end of a December day, buffeting with traffic and weary people and slanting rain and a chilly wind.

It didn't feel safe. Louis looked down at his lamb-that-wasn't-a-lamb and saw that it had somehow got scrunched. He tried to smooth the creases, and a skittering gust caught it and flung it into a puddle.

'Iffen!' cried Louis, and rushed to pick it up.

Now it wasn't a lamb, and it wasn't Iffen either. It was a gritty, woolly, wet-papery nothing. Even so, Louis couldn't quite throw it away. He didn't know what to do. He hunched his jacket tight around him and stuffed his handful of nothing in his pocket.

His fingers met ivy leaves, cool and smooth. They helped Louis think. He thought, *Home.*

Which way is home? wondered Louis, clutching his leaves, and then, like a series of stepping stones, he knew.

Past the street bin where Amit got his head stuck and the fire brigade had to get him out. Past the lamp post with its horrible graffiti picture of a skull. Up to the crossing where Esmé always held his arm and said, 'Wait! Wait for green!'

Louis waited for green, crossed safely to the middle, waited again and reached the other side. The next landmark was the vet's, which was easy to spot because it had silver metal animals all along the railings – cat, rabbit, tortoise, dog, parrot – and Louis knew he was going to be all right, because there was Abi's bus stop and a minute later the cooking smell from the noodle shop. Now, just round the corner, the ivy house waited.

It was suddenly very quiet.

All along the street, the shadows were deep behind parked cars and walls and entrances. Curtains were closed across windows. Louis peered into the gloom. Was the Narnia lamp on?

No.

So no one is home, thought Louis. *The door will be locked.* A question repeated over and over, in his head: *What'll I do? What'll I do?*

As he came closer to the house, he wondered some more what he would do. There was a small movement in their scruffy hedge: pause, move again, pause.

Iffen? wondered Louis.

Perhaps it was just a bird.

Please . . . not Iffen.

The yews around the old church held darkness like a mantle. Louis watched them out of the corner of one eye. Then another sound came, halfway between a cough and an exclamation.

Tcha!

Louis' heart jumped.

He heard a roosting pigeon rise from the yew trees, shrieking and clapping in alarm. He pictured thorn-black claws, and fangs as long as his finger. He remembered the great weight of Iffen's silent velvet tread, and panic seized him.

Tcha! he heard again, closer, and a rustle like heavy silk.

Louis ran, leaping for the doorstep. 'Not now! Not now!' he gasped, as he pounded with his fists. 'Not now! Somebody! Somebody!' And then, beyond all hope, the door was opened, and he tumbled inside, gasping, shaking and yet again in tears. Tears not just of loneliness, but of shame and fear and temper, because he had run away from his friend at last.

'Iffen, Iffen, Iffen!' sobbed Louis, but he leaned against the door to hold it shut.

A little earlier that same afternoon, Max had met Abi as she climbed off her bus. After the art college he'd gone back to school to collect his bike and now he was pushing it, with Esmé's enormous portfolio balanced on the handlebars.

'You got it!' Abi exclaimed as soon as she saw what he was carrying.

'Yep.'

'Didn't Esmé mind?'

'I didn't see her. She'd already handed it in to Danny's mum, so I had to . . . had to nick it!'

'Nick it?'

'What else could I do? We'll just have to put it out of sight when she comes back with Louis.'

'You were right to take it,' admitted Abi. 'We have to have it. And we've got to think quickly of a way to use it, before Iffen comes again.' She looked nervously over her shoulder as she spoke. All at once the street seemed very long.

'Would it . . . he . . . come if Louis wasn't there?' asked Max.

'I don't know,' said Abi, walking more quickly, almost running. 'Perhaps.'

'Let's not put any lights on when we get in.'

'Why not?'

'So it doesn't look like anyone's home if he's watching the house.'

The thought of Iffen watching the house was so uncomfortable that Abi began to talk very fast to distract herself.

'I've been thinking all day about how we could get him to go back. Iffen, I mean. I'm sure it's possible, because it happened with an animal once before.'

Max stopped pushing his bike to look at her in amazement and ask what she was talking about.

'Do you remember I told you about the raft in the book? There was a parrot on that raft, a tame parrot. I saw it clearly. It flew towards me, just as Louis called my name, and then swerved away again. I think Louis saw it, just for a moment. I remember he asked me, "What was that green?" So if the parrot could come out of a book, and then go back in, Iffen should be able to do the same . . . I hope. What colour eyes do lions and panthers have in the dark?'

'What?'

'I just wondered if you knew.'

'No I don't. Why are you scaring yourself?'

'I'm not.'

'Well, you're scaring me! Hurry up! Let's get inside.'

They had reached the house. Abi fumbled for her door key.

192

If she'd taken a minute longer and looked back, she'd have seen Louis behind them, just turning the corner. But she didn't do that. She found the key quickly, unlocked the door and stood aside to let Max go in with his bike.

'You first,' said Max calmly, but he followed behind her fast enough, and closed the door very swiftly.

'Dump your bike and bring Esmé's book into the rocking-horse room,' said Abi. 'We'll have some light from the street lamp in there.'

Max obeyed, and followed her into the room, pale in its dust sheets, lit from outside, not dark but not light, with its shadowed grey walls.

A cave of a room.

Together, he and Abi put the book on the sofa, and had already opened it, turned past the maps and the bison, and the outlines of the bears. They had come to a page of horses when the pounding began on the door.

For a moment they stared at each other in shock. Then Abi spun round to go to the window, and Max grabbed her back.

'Don't show yourself!' he whispered, and then went quickly forward, slipping around the room until he reached a place where it was possible to see out to the doorstep.

The hammering came again, with shrieks.

'It's Louis!' exclaimed Max suddenly, and ran to the front door.

Louis shot inside, slammed it shut, and leaned on it. 'Iffen, Iffen, Iffen!' he gasped between sobs.

'Louis, don't!' said Abi, dismayed. 'Iffen's not here. It's OK. Why isn't Esmé with you?'

Louis wept on.

'Louis, stop it!' said Max, taking him by his shoulders. 'Look at me! Talk to me! Did you come back on your own?'

Louis nodded.

'All the way from After-school Club?'

He nodded again.

'They'll be going mad!' said Max. 'They'll call the police if we don't tell them he's OK . . .'

'I've got their number,' said Abi. She was already texting **Louis Valentine home safe** to Theo, the After-school Club and Esmé. 'There! Sent! Louis, what frightened you just now?'

Louis blubbered and snuffled into his sleeve.

'You have to tell us what happened, Lou!' said Max, but Louis shook his head and wouldn't, until Abi, inspired, said, 'Come into the rocking-horse room. I'm going to jump you up on to Rocky.'

That stopped the floods. Louis wobbled for a moment, rubbed his eyes and looked up at Abi in surprise.

'You said I couldn't.'

'I've changed my mind,' said Abi. 'Blow your nose properly . . . That's a dust sheet! Oh, never mind. There! Hold on tight! OK?'

Louis managed a shaky smile as Abi started Rocky moving, his street-lamp shadow rocking too, huge against the white-sheeted sofa.

'Now tell us why you were in such a state,' said Max.

'Howling and hammering on the door like that. What frightened you?'

'Did you see Iffen?' asked Abi.

'No,' said Louis, feeling much better now that he was home with Abi and Max, and actually riding Rocky at last. 'Why've you got Esmé's book?'

'Louis, you know how Iffen isn't ordinary? He's real, like the snow and the shell, but he's magic too. The way Theo can't see him. The way he grew so quickly. We talked about it, didn't we?'

'Yes.'

'And I said I thought he'd come out of a book and said you hadn't read any books.'

'I haven't.'

'But books have pictures as well as words. You remember Max in your room yesterday? All covered in chalk dust? After he got you down the ivy, and we pushed the door open, and Iffen jumped out of the window?'

Louis nodded.

'That chalk dust was from the world Esmé drew in her art book. Max saw it. He was there. He told us about seeing the animals running.'

'Yes,' said Louis.

'Louis,' said Max, joining in. 'It was a big herd of bison, young ones and old ones, so close I could feel the ground shaking. The track was dry and there was chalk dust like a cloud and after they'd passed me I saw why they were running like that.'

195

'Why were they?'

'There were three big cats hunting them. Two running alongside, one behind, I saw them just for a moment, outlined in the dust. Big cats, lion-sized, like Iffen.'

'Like Iffen?' repeated Louis in a suddenly husky voice.

'Yes. Big, like him. Powerful. Not spotted, but big cats like him.'

'Were you scared?'

'There wasn't time to be scared.'

'You've seen Esmé's art book dozens of times,' said Abi. 'That's where he's come from, I'm sure. And he's got so big. You've got to let him go back, Louis.'

Outside and alone, Louis had been terrified at the thought of Iffen in the dark. Inside, his fear had faded. 'I love him big,' he said obstinately, not ceasing to rock. 'When he gets bigger, I love him bigger.'

'He's wild,' said Max. 'He's meant to be wild. This is his world. Look!'

He began turning the pages of Esmé's portfolio. In the dimly lit, pale room, Louis' shadow rocked across an outline of a stag, a bison with a lowered head, more horses, a herd of running antelope.

'That's where he belongs,' said Max. 'Abi's right – you know she is. You have to let him go. We've only got Esmé's book for a little while. I've got to take it back. Listen, I've been thinking, if we put it in your room, with the window wide open, maybe with some food around . . . Will you do something really brave?'

'What?'

'Call him.'

'Call him?' Louis' voice went very high and not at all brave, and his rocking became suddenly frantic. 'Call him? On my own?'

'No! No!' said Abi. 'We'd stay with you, right beside you.'

'And as soon as we hear him coming we'll get outside and block the door,' said Max. 'Wedge it. We'll have things ready. There's that blanket chest . . .'

Max's voice stopped, like a radio switched off. He stood quite still, staring at the window. Nothing about him moved except the pupils of his eyes. They dilated into wideness.

'What?' asked Abi, puzzled, and then she saw as well.

Iffen.

Iffen had arrived.

Iffen's wild, watching face was staring in at the window. Exactly where Max had first seen Esmé, but ten times larger, filling the whole space. His great amber eyes were gazing into the dimly lit cave of a room, at the huge image of running deer and the rocking shadow over them. It was an alert, hunting gaze.

Terror gripped Max, and it held Abi, too, with her heart flopping like a caught fish, hard against her ribcage.

Only Louis moved.

Louis forgot all plans and all fears, and saw only his dear Iffen, shut out in the night, and he jumped down from Rocky so quickly he left his shadow still rocking behind him, and pushed open the window wide in welcome.

'Iffen!' he exclaimed in delight.

'*Tcha!*' said Iffen, and for the last time Louis felt the rough silken fur, the lithe, muscled warmth, and then Iffen surged past, and in a lion spring sailed clear over Rocky and streamed in dark outlines and charcoal blots and gold and grey amongst the running herd and the rocking shadows, and vanished.

'Wait!' screeched Louis, and he plunged after Iffen, and tumbled through thirty thousand years, and after him came Abi and Max.

Then the room was empty. Iffen was gone, and Louis was gone. Max and Abi were gone. There was nothing left except the smell of green magic, and Rocky and his shadow moving more and more slowly.

Max and Abi landed in a heap amongst long grass. Frightened crickets sprayed away like an explosion of green sparks. A little distance from them, Louis stood on narrow white track, squinting into the sunlight. Much further away, where the chalk cliffs rose, a great spotted cat leaped from ledge to ledge, higher and higher, until it was almost out of sight.

Suddenly Louis began running, heading across the valley.

'Louis!' shouted Abi. Her voice was thin and empty, like a voice in a dream, but Louis must have heard, because he hesitated long enough to give Max time to sprint and grab him. It seemed to Abi then that Louis' shrieks of protest woke the whole sun-flooded landscape. There were movements, just out of sight, and there was the feel of watching eyes. Most of all there was the knowledge of being in a place they should not be.

And, Abi realized, as she ran to join the boys, they had left behind an empty house.

There was no one at home to call them back.

'Iffen!' screeched Louis, and the tiny, moving shape on the distant chalk cliff seemed to pause.

'Louis, no!' said Abi. 'Please be quiet! Hold my hand! Max, there's no one home!'

But even as she spoke, a noise grew all around them, faint, and then louder, a familiar sound: the rustling of green ivy.

Then a great crash, Max's bike tumbling down in the hall.

Wind above the chimney in the rocking-horse room.

Rocky's slow rhythmic creak . . . creak . . . creak.

The house was calling them back.

It was as if the landscape withdrew. The ground felt insubstantial. The colours leached away, and with them the heat and the cricket sounds. It seemed to Abi that, above all things, she must hang on to Louis. Max had hold of him too, and with his other hand he was gripping the top of Abi's arm so tightly that it hurt.

Rocky came to rest, a painted shape in the thin light from the lamp outside in the street. Cold December air blew through the open window. They could smell the ivy and the dust sheets and the soot from the chimney, and it was over.

Max was the first to move, and he was very fast. He let go of Abi and Louis, grabbed Esmé's book, closed it shut and gathered it up – antelope, bison, dust, ancient chalk, bears, lions, great spotted cat and the small bright prints of Louis' hand.

'I've got to take it back,' he said.

'No!' begged Louis. 'Not yet! Not yet!' but Max was already gone, and Abi and Louis were alone. They gazed around like travellers after a great journey, half bewildered, limp, blinking to see once more the unbelievable familiar doors and walls and windows of home.

'The window,' said Abi, and closed it shut.

'I wish I hadn't opened it,' wailed Louis. 'Iffen! Iffen! Why did I open it?'

'Because you loved him,' said Abi. 'That's why.'

Max reached Danny's house in record time, texting on the way. Danny was watching out for him from his bedroom window.

'Can you come and get this without your mum seeing?' called Max in a hoarse sort of whisper.

'Mate,' said Danny, who had been waiting for this moment, 'I can do better than that.'

Then from the window fell Danny's old Spider-Man duvet cover, attached to a knotted rope made entirely of socks. All Max had to do was post the book inside and watch as it was hauled up, and out of sight.

'Impressed?' asked Danny, reappearing. 'Now bash on the door, and when she answers keep her talking while I sneak down and put this in the kitchen with the rest. She's got them all piled up on the table.'

He gave Max a double thumbs-up and disappeared. Max obediently bashed on the door, there were footsteps and then

Danny's mother exclaiming, 'It's Max! Don't stand there in the dark, Max! Come in this minute! I'm making soup. Danny!' she called over her shoulder. 'Max is here! Have you all got on well with my lovely Esmé, Max? Isn't it a shame she's leaving so soon? I bet Louis will be pleased to have Polly back, though! Are you all rushing around tidying?'

'Tidying?' asked Max weakly. 'Yes. I suppose.'

He did suppose returning a thirty-thousand-year-old full-grown spotted mountain lion to its rightful place in time might be called a sort of tidying.

'I don't know why Danny's taking so long! Now, Max, could you manage a Christmas tree? One of Danny's brothers is selling Christmas trees this month, and we've got all the not-quite-straight ones stacked up by the wheelie bins. There's absolutely nothing wrong with them. It does seem a waste. Could you carry it, do you think? Oh, here's Danny at last!'

'Stop trying to give everyone who knocks on the door bent Christmas trees, Mum,' said Danny. 'It's embarrassing. All right, Max?'

'All right,' said Max. 'I just came to say thanks for the . . . for . . . for the sock thing.'

'Sock thing?' asked Danny's mum, and then there was an erupting, hissing sound from the kitchen. 'Soup!' she cried and ran.

Danny and Max sighed with relief.

'The book's back in the pile,' said Danny. 'Did you get whatever it was fixed where it should be?'

'Yeah. In the end. Thanks. Danny?'

201

'What's up?'

'I had a text from Esmé just now, on the way here. It said, Can you manage without me?'

'Mate, you do know she was probably, almost certainly, talking about babysitting your brother?'

'Yeah, she was. I do know that. Because he left school without her and we had to message to say he was safe home. It's what I replied I wanted to ask you about.'

'Shoot!' said Danny, sticking his thumbs in his belt and leaning back like a cowboy.

'I sent back, Yes, but not forever. In French.'

'In French?'

'Yep.'

'How'd you manage that?'

'Google Translate. So d'you think it was a bad move?'

'I think it was brilliant,' said Danny. 'Google Translate! Saves all that messing about with dictionaries.'

'I mean saying it.'

'I think that was brilliant too.'

'Thanks,' said Max, and meant it. 'I'd better go. Thanks.'

'Wait!' said Danny, and pushed something into his hand.

It was Max's lost Nike trainers in a carrier bag. 'Cleaned,' said Danny. 'Washed the laces, even. OK?'

'OK,' said Max, quite overwhelmed, and on his way out he chose the biggest bent Christmas tree, balanced it on his shoulder, took the bag in his other hand, and set off for home.

It was a long and prickly journey, but at last he arrived, wrestled his tree through the front door, dragged it into the rocking-horse room, propped it silently in the window and slumped down beside Abi and Louis, now both fast asleep on the sofa. He thought he would wait quietly until they woke up, but after the day that had just happened and the night on the stairs before, it wasn't very long until he was asleep as well. He woke up to the smell of hot chocolate and Theo folding dust sheets and humming. 'Hello, Max. Abi. I see we have a Christmas tree. Louis, I need a word . . .'

'Not now,' said Louis, and closed his eyes again.

Chapter Twenty-one

The school term ended, and Esmé went back to France. For a day or two Max wandered around feeling lost. He didn't know where Esmé was – sometimes it felt as if he didn't know to the nearest thirty thousand years. At first there seemed to be no cure for this. The book from the library with pictures of the Chauvet Cave didn't help. Writing poems in English and putting them into Google Translate, and then distrustfully looking up all the words in a dictionary afterwards, didn't help either.

Danny helped. Danny said, after a day or two of this moping, 'Mate, listen! Next summer, is there any reason – apart from the parents, we'll talk them round – why we shouldn't go hitchhiking in France for a few weeks? Maybe say hello?'

Max cheered up a lot at this suggestion and said he could see no reason at all (apart from the parents, and there was months to talk them round), and then he thought a bit longer and asked, 'But what about money?'

Danny said money would not be a problem if they relaunched the bike-repair and car-cleaning business as soon as possible. In the great collecting of equipment that followed, of buckled wheels and dirty sponges and chains and cables and graphite lubricant, Max began to feel very much better. With the setting up of a proper accounts system with a petty-cash box and a book with expenses and income listed, and a biro tied on with string, he improved even more. He began practising hair styles and cool, but non-smiling, expressions for passport photos. He and Danny both agreed not to mention it to the parents till they'd got the first hundred pounds together. Max had the genius idea of selling car-cleaning vouchers as Christmas gifts. Theo bought two straight away, one as a thank you for his chimney-sweeping friend, one for Polly.

Theo could not stop smiling because Polly was coming back.

'You said that before,' said Louis accusingly. 'You always say it and she never, ever comes.'

Louis was in an empty, needy, grumpy mood. Theo had nit-combed him. Max and Danny had told him in blunt words that he was underage for bike repair and car cleaning, and they would only reconsider his application in six years' time if he shut up going on about it now. Granny Grace had sent Abi a soft, soft beanie, knitted in shades of gold. Louis had been so jealous when she opened it that he'd cried. He was sick of the world. His heart ached at the sight of the rips in his rug. He didn't even have his polishing to do because the rocking-horse room was finished.

It looked wonderful. The sheets were gathered up, there

were curtains in the window and a fireguard over a real fire in the hearth. Max's tree was still bare and dark, waiting till Polly came home.

It was time to decorate the house for Christmas.

Abi took charge. They began in the rocking-horse room with paper snowflakes, gold and silver bells, and great strands of ivy. Rocky had a garland of ivy, and there was another hung on the door. Its green stars were Esmé to Max, ever since she'd untangled the leaf from his hair and tucked it behind her ear. Wherever she was, she was still close enough to affect the beat of his heart. His screen saver now was a map of France, and the day before he'd sent her a text:

Très Cool Noël, Esmé!

Mx

And, straight away, one had come back:

Très Cool Noël à toi aussi!

x

He'd shown it to Abi, and mentioned the hitchhiking idea. Abi had said, 'Brilliant,' and that she'd back him up if he needed. She was a lot more use than Danny's big brothers, who'd unanimously agreed he was mad.

She was being very bossy about the snowflakes and bells, but Max didn't mind at all.

'Wow, looking good!' Theo exclaimed when he came in to

see how they were all getting on. 'Now, I've got to go out to pick something up . . .' He nodded at Max and Abi, and they nodded back and gave each other significant and secret looks over Louis' head. '*So*,' Theo continued, 'no climbing the walls, no biking down stairs, no frostbite, no touching the fire – Louis, that's you! Be good, and I'll bring us back pizza.'

Louis, who was slumped gloomily on Rocky not helping with anything, said he couldn't touch the fire because they'd put it in a cage and he didn't like pizza any more.

'What *do* you like?' asked Theo, and Louis said, 'Nothing, only rocking,' and he rocked very slowly, with his face half buried in Rocky's garland. The leaves were Iffen again, pouring through the window in his cloak of crushed green scent, but Iffen was gone and the magic was gone too. Esmé was gone, Mrs Puddock was gone, recent extensive investigation had shown that even the black from his nose was gone, and Louis was feeling deserted.

Theo looked at him dubiously and said, 'Perhaps you should come with me. Only you might have to wait around quite a while, and you hate that.'

'And Abi and Max would do things without me,' said Louis.

'True,' agreed Theo.

'I'll come if I can bring Rocky, and if Abi and Max promise not to do anything good till I come back,' offered Louis.

'Totally unreasonable,' said Theo. 'Impossible. No room for negotiation at all.'

'What does that mean?' demanded Louis.

'*No!*' said Theo, Abi and Max altogether, and Abi added to Theo, 'Just go, in case . . .'

'In case, what?' asked Louis.

'Traffic,' said Abi vaguely, but behind Louis' back she mouthed to Theo, 'in case it's early!'

'Much more likely to be late,' said Theo.

'What's more likely to be late?' demanded Louis.

'Me,' said Theo. 'I'll be late, if I don't get going. Max, Abi, sure you'll be okay? I could take him, but . . .'

'He'd be a nightmare,' said Max, and Abi nodded in agreement.

'Text,' ordered Max, indicating his mobile phone. 'When . . .'

'I will,' said Theo, beaming so cheerfully that Louis noticed and lifted his sad head to say no one cared about him and he didn't love any of them, and at that moment the letter box rattled. Abi jumped up as if it was something she'd been waiting for and rushed out of the room. She came back a minute later with a pale blue envelope from Granny Grace and showed it to Theo.

Theo touched two fingers to his lips and bowed to Abi. Abi held the letter out to Louis, and said, 'Look!'

'Why?' asked Louis suspiciously.

'Because it's got your name on.'

'No it hasn't,' said Louis, turning his face away.

'Don't be pathetic, Louis!' ordered Max, so Louis looked after all, and it was true. There was his name.

'Open it,' said Max.

Louis, who had not forgotten the other letter he had opened from Granny Grace, looked at Abi.

'Open it,' said Abi, so Louis took the envelope and tore open the top very carefully, so as not to spoil the lovely stamps, and found a folded sheet of blue paper.

His own private letter from Granny Grace.

Louis' face began to glow, as if he'd opened a small package of fresh Jamaican sunshine. He whispered to Rocky, 'It's true.'

Theo made a finger circle sign of perfection to Abi, gave a thumbs-up to Max and tiptoed out of the room.

'Let's hear what she says, then,' said Max.

The handwriting on the blue paper reminded Abi of her own learning-to-read days, each letter carefully separated. However, Granny Grace didn't believe in making things too easy. Just as when Abi was learning to read, she had included long words and commas, right from the start.

'Shout if you need help,' said Abi, but Louis, for the first words at least, didn't need help.

'*My sweet Louis*,' he read aloud, and paused to look at Abi, and she saw his eyes were already alight with a silver shine of intense happiness.

'*My sweet Louis*,' he repeated. '*I have in front of me your s-m . . . sm . . . iling . . . smiling face in my . . . in my . . . in my p-h . . . my . . .*'

'*Photograph*,' read Abi for him, '*of the wedding . . .*'

'I did smile!' agreed Louis, nodding. 'I remember! I smiled extra because you and Max wouldn't. I can read this now, listen! *My sweet Louis, I have in front of me your smiling face in my photograph from the wedding. Now, Louis, Ab . . . Ab . . .*'

'*Abigail,*' said Abigail. 'That's me!'

'What?'

'Abigail is me. I am Abigail.'

'Why are you?'

'It's my name.'

'Fancy not knowing your own sister's name,' remarked Max from his place by the window where the phone signal was best and he could see right down the street.

'*. . . Abigail tells me how you do not read your school books. I hope so much that she is . . . is . . .*'

Louis was stuck again.

'*Mistaken,*' read Abi.

'*I hope you like school, Louis. I and my three sisters loved our school. We did not miss a day . . .*'

'*Not even when the storm rains took away our small bridge across the river,*' recited Abi. '*We put our school books on our heads and we waded across that river and we were not late!*'

'How do you know it says that?' demanded Louis.

'Does it?'

'Yes,' said Max, who could read upside-down writing as easily as right way up.

'I'm going to read the rest myself,' said Louis. 'So don't help!

'*If you had been with us, Louis, I think you would have done the same . . .* Yes I would! I'd have swimmed! Easy.'

'Swum,' said Max severely. 'Don't talk baby!'

'It wasn't really a swimming river,' said Abi. 'It was a little tiny trickle. I've seen pictures. Go on. Read some more.'

'*I have sent you a flower* . . . Oh! Oh!' Louis gasped with delight, and scrabbled in the envelope. 'I've got it! Here! . . . *Is it purple or blue? It comes from the tree I like best. Now, Louis, please write back soon to your loving Granny Grace.*'

He'd done it, the whole letter, with terrible words like 'smiling' and 'photograph' and 'purple'. No paper-covered schoolbook had ever flung such obstacles in his path. But he hadn't fallen – he'd leaped over them. He panted like a boy at the end of a race. He looked at Abi, and said, 'For me from Granny Grace!'

'Yes,' said Abi.

'This is my letter,' gloated Louis. 'And this is my flower.'

'Purple or blue?' asked Max.

Louis bent over the flower, shut his eyes, breathed in deep, looked again and laughed out loud. 'I know, I know, I know!' he said. 'Paper! I need paper!'

'What for?' asked Max, but Abi understood and fetched him her own airmail pad.

Dear Granny Grace –

Louis paused to wipe his nose on his hand.

This is my letter. Abi helped. Max helped.

It was easiest, Louis found, to write on the floor with the paper tipped sideways and the pencil clutched to his heart.

The flower is purple –

Or was it? Was it?

AND pink AND blue.

212

I love you –
From your sweet Louis.

It had taken a long time. The whole morning had passed. Most of Abi's paper was gone. Two pencils had been ground down to stumps. Many times Max had checked his phone; after the last he caught Abi's eye and nodded and held it up so that she could read the message on the screen.

'At last,' said Abi, and Louis, thinking she was referring to his letter, agreed, 'At last.'

The blue and purple flower was limp. Louis' fingers were exhausted. He flapped them to uncramp them, while Abi found an envelope and wrote out the address. He watched her anxiously.

'Will she like it?' he asked. 'Is it enough?'

It didn't feel enough. It didn't say anything about Iffen. The hugeness of Iffen, and knowing Iffen and losing Iffen. It didn't say anything about the green magic that had swept through the house and bowled them over and changed their world, and fixed it, and given it back again.

Nevertheless, it was words on paper. It opened a door, it made a friend, it told a story.

Louis looked at it. He turned it over and felt the back, where his pencil had left patterns in runey ridges. He looked at the front again, and it was even better than he remembered. He sniffed it and thought he found the faintest trace of Iffen, whom one day he would find again, when he discovered where to look.

'Where did it all come from?' he asked Abi, and she knew at once what he meant.

Iffen, prowling among the shadow lines between real and unreal. The rocking-horse room a cave. The way that Rocky's shadow had brought to life a herd of running deer. The worlds to be found in words and pictures.

'It came out of books,' said Abi, handing him the envelope. 'I think you'd better start reading. And you should put in an ivy leaf.'

AUTHOR'S NOTE

The Chauvet Cave, in the Ardèche region of France, contains a collection of Stone Age cave art that is over thirty thousand years old. It is – and I think always has been – closed to the public, in order to protect it from deterioration, as happened with the cave art in Lascaux, but there are books about it, and a French documentary film. The drawings are of animals, wonderfully lifelike. There are bison, antelope, bears, horses, hyena, panthers, mammoths, birds, reindeer, lions . . .

. . . and one spotted cat.

HM
January 2019

ACKNOWLEDGEMENTS

This book owes a great deal to the wisdom and encouragement of three wonderful editors: Venetia Gosling (Pan Macmillan), Karen Wojtyla (Simon & Schuster Children's Books) and Jasmine Richards (StoryMix). My agent extraordinaire, Molly Ker Hawn, got the jokes with admirable speed, Dawn Cooper did the gorgeous cover art and Bella was the first reader.

Thank you so much to all of you.

H x

(All the mistakes were made by me with no help from anyone because I am so good at it.)

ABOUT THE AUTHOR

Hilary McKay is the critically-acclaimed author of many children's novels, several of which have won awards, most notably *The Skylarks' War*, which won the Costa Children's Book Award. Hilary also won the *Guardian* Children's Fiction Prize for her first novel, *The Exiles*, and the Whitbread Award (now the Costa) for *Saffy's Angel*.

She studied Botany and Zoology at the University of St Andrews, and worked as a biochemist before the draw of the pen became too strong and she decided to become a full-time writer. Hilary lives in Derbyshire with her family.

'Beautifully written, witty, observant . . .
Merits a place in the canon of children's classics'
The Sunday Times Children's Book of the Year

Winner of the Costa Children's Book Award 2018